HARLEQUIN®

Leslie Kelly
Jennifer LaBrecque

BLAZING BEDTIME STORIES
{ VOLUME V }

The best fantasies
are the ones that come true...

Blaze™

The ultimate destination for red-hot reads…

AVAILABLE NOW:

#537 BLAZING BEDTIME STORIES, VOLUME V
Bedtime Stories
Leslie Kelly and Jennifer LaBrecque

#538 SPONTANEOUS
Brenda Jackson

#539 SURPRISE ME…
The Wrong Bed: Again and Again
Isabel Sharpe

#540 LED INTO TEMPTATION
Twice Forbidden
Cara Summers

#541 LONG SUMMER NIGHTS
Where You Least Expect It
Kathleen O'Reilly

#542 MAKE YOUR MOVE
Samantha Hunter

ISBN-13:978-0-373-79541-3

50499

EAN

HBATMIFC0510

ABOUT THE AUTHORS

Leslie Kelly has written more than two dozen books and novellas for Harlequin Blaze, Temptation and HQN Books. Known for her sparkling dialogue, fun characters and depth of emotion, her books have been honored with numerous awards, including a National Readers' Choice Award and three nominations for the RWA RITA® Award. Leslie resides in Maryland with her own romantic hero, Bruce, and their three daughters. Visit her online at www.lesliekelly.com, or at her alter-ego's site, www.authorleslieparrish.com.

After a varied career path that included barbecue-joint waitress, corporate number-cruncher and bug-business maven, **Jennifer LaBrecque** has found her true calling writing contemporary romance. Named 2001 Notable New Author of the Year and 2002 winner of the prestigious Maggie Award for Excellence, she is also a two-time RITA® Award finalist. Jennifer lives in suburban Atlanta.

Leslie Kelly
Jennifer LaBrecque

BLAZING BEDTIME STORIES, VOLUME V

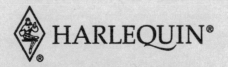

HARLEQUIN®

TORONTO • NEW YORK • LONDON
AMSTERDAM • PARIS • SYDNEY • HAMBURG
STOCKHOLM • ATHENS • TOKYO • MILAN • MADRID
PRAGUE • WARSAW • BUDAPEST • AUCKLAND

ISBN-13: 978-0-373-79541-3

BLAZING BEDTIME STORIES, VOLUME V
Copyright © 2010 by Harlequin Books S.A.

The publisher acknowledges the copyright holders of the individual works as follows:

A PRINCE OF A GUY
Copyright © 2010 by Leslie Kelly

GOLDIE AND THE THREE BROTHERS
Copyright © 2010 by Jennifer LaBrecque

PLEASE RECYCLE • THIS PRODUCT IS RECYCLABLE •

Recycling programs for this product may not exist in your area.

This edition published by arrangement with Harlequin Books S.A.

For questions and comments about the quality of this book please contact us at Customer_eCare@Harlequin.ca.

® and TM are trademarks of the publisher. Trademarks indicated with ® are registered in the United States Patent and Trademark Office, the Canadian Trade Marks Office and in other countries.

www.eHarlequin.com

Printed in U.S.A.

CONTENTS

To the Brothers Grimm, Hans Christian Anderson, Mark Twain (author of the original *The Prince and the Pauper*) and all the other wonderful storytellers who have given us fairy tales, fables and bedtime stories to pass down through the generations.

A PRINCE OF A GUY
Leslie Kelly

Prologue

ONCE UPON A TIME, there lived a handsome prince who would much rather have been born a princess. He hated jousting and war, preferring to be fought over than to fight. He liked tiaras more than crowns and was better at disco dancing than the waltz.

One day, after hearing of a city that boasted a bridge with golden gates, and a rainbow parade, he made his way to a wondrous place called San Francisco and found his heart's true desire.

The club scene.

Unfortunately, his mother, the wicked queen, was determined that her son should come home and be crowned king. So she sent for the most powerful Amazon warrior in the land. Surely such a woman, trained from childhood in the art of war, would have no trouble finding the prince and forcing him to return. Nor would she fall prey to any feminine weaknesses and develop any personal feelings for a fussy runaway.

But his super-sexy double?

Well, that was a whole other story….

1

HAVING BEEN TRAINED to believe it was her duty, and a great honor, to die protecting a member of the royal family, Olivia Vanderbrook tried very hard not to dislike her queen.

The bitch didn't make it easy.

Queen Verona, the dowager who had ruled the kingdom of Grand Falls for sixteen years, since the death of her husband, was the most unpleasant person Olivia had ever known. The jewels dripping from every pudgy finger might sparkle, but the woman's true personality couldn't be brightened with all the gold in Elatyria.

Verona—once called Fair Verona—was petty and vain. Greedy and hungry for wealth. Impatient and capricious, she would hold a grudge for a hundred years after she was put in her grave.

To top it all off, she had truly awful taste in clothes. Olivia might always wear a simple black-leather uniform, designed for free movement in battle, but she knew a really bad dress when she saw one. Made with yards of heavy fabric and gaudy trimmings, the queen's ugly gowns would look better on that nudist emperor who liked prancing about his kingdom without a stitch on.

Despite all that, Olivia knew she should admire the woman. In this man's world, Verona had managed to defeat enemies who wanted to wrest the kingdom away from her young son, heir to the throne. She had become renowned for her shrewd dealings and her ruthless nature. Though not loved, Verona was feared and respected by all her subjects. Well, feared, anyway.

So as the captain of the all-female, Amazonian Royal Guard, Olivia should have been down with all of that. Women-supreme, chicks rule. Power to the va-jay-jay.

But no. As she stood in one of the queen's private receiving rooms, her head slightly bowed, feet apart, the butt of her longbow braced between them, she could only think it was a shame the king had died all those years ago, rather than his spiteful wife.

Olivia's father and the late king had been close friends. She remembered the former ruler as a kind man who had never ordered the head lopped off even the most saucy peasant. Renowned for his merry nature, he'd had a deep belly laugh and blew huge smoke rings from his pipe. He'd enjoyed playing chase-the-chambermaid, and so loved to dance that he kept a trio of fiddlers on call at all times.

Looking on him as an uncle, Olivia remembered anxiously awaiting his royal visits to her family's estate. He'd always brought wonderful presents for the Vanderbrook children. Frilly dolls and bows for her sisters. Books for her studious brother.

And weapons and miniaturized suits of armor for Olivia.

When she'd been but a child, the king had recognized in Olivia the same fighting spirit her most famous ancestor—her great-great-great-grandmother—had, a woman who'd been the leader of the last free-roaming Amazon band. The king had encouraged Olivia to join the Guard, and urged her parents to let her.

Considering they had several other daughters to marry off, and one studious, serious son who showed no interest in soldiering, Olivia's parents hadn't fought the idea. Every family needed a warrior—theirs would just be their second-oldest girl rather than their only boy. That she would be giving up a normal life—husband, family and everything else—hadn't bothered her, or them, one bit. Because nobody had ever assumed she'd wanted them.

Everyone had known her destiny, and none had been surprised she'd risen through the ranks to achieve the highest rank—Captain of the Guard—by her twenty-eighth year. Her only regret was that the old king, who'd so encouraged her, hadn't lived to see it.

Oh, yes, if he were still her monarch, the idea of laying down her life would be a whole lot easier to swallow.

For Queen Verona, though? Not so much.

"Ahh, there you are, Captain," the queen said, imperious as she swept into the private chamber where Olivia had been kept waiting at attention for nearly an hour.

"Greetings, Your Majesty," Olivia said, her head still down. Nobody looked the queen directly in the eye unless invited.

The queen draped herself across a chaise lounge, spreading out the skirt of her puce-colored brocade gown. Plucking off a piece of lint, she behaved like she had not a care in the world.

Olivia wasn't fooled. The queen was upset—the bulging veins in her neck and the ham-hock fisting of her hands made it clear. Knowing better than to speak until addressed, she didn't ask why.

"I have an important mission for you. A secret mission."

"I am grateful for your confidence in me, Majesty."

"You have undoubtedly heard that my son, Prince Ruprecht, is out on the continent, sowing his oats before his coronation."

Olivia nodded once. Everyone knew that the gay prince

had gone off for one last romp before assuming the mantle of king. All of Grand Falls hoped that during his travels, he'd find a princess to wed. He had proved very picky about choosing a bride.

"Well," the queen said, "it's not true."

Though startled, Olivia managed to avoid showing it.

"In fact, the prince has…left. Without our blessing."

"Left, Your Majesty? Do you mean he has, er, run away?" It was a ridiculous way to put it since the prince was a man of nearly thirty years. Though, to be honest, he didn't act much like a man. Well, not the way Olivia thought a real man should act.

"Yes," the woman admitted. "Call it what you want. He got it in his head to go over *there* before taking his place as king."

Over *there*. Olivia sucked in a surprised breath. Usually, the other place was only spoken of in whispers or cautionary bedtime stories to children. *Be good, or you'll be sent over* there *to work in a fast food restaurant!* Whatever that was.

Just to be sure, she asked, "You mean, Earth?"

"Yes, of course I mean Earth!"

Earth, the flipside of reality. The darker reflection of her own world.

Earth, whose inhabitants believed everything about Elatyria was simply a fairy tale, a bedtime story—as if they were amusing, insignificant and to be laughed at.

She'd been there. She didn't like it.

"His note promised he would be back well in time for his coronation, on his birthday, but I haven't heard one single word from him in months."

A note. Great Athena's ghost, the future king had left a note and traipsed away like a moody little princess. "I see."

The queen stopped pacing. Her frown dropped her

jowls almost down to her shoulders. "I blame that awful Penelope Mayfair!"

That would be Queen Penelope, newly arrived and crowned head of the neighboring kingdom of Riverdale. She'd been raised on the Earth side, from what Olivia understood.

"She filled Ruprecht's head with silly prattle of some city with a golden bridge and a parade of people who love rainbows!"

"That is where he went? To this city with a golden bridge?"

"Yes. It's in a place called California." The queen came closer, to within a few steps. Without warning, she reached out and grabbed Olivia's chin, lifting Olivia's face to look her in the eye. "You must go find him. And bring him back here."

"Majesty, what if the prince doesn't wish to return?"

"Then toss him in a sack and bring him anyway!"

Olivia swallowed. Lay violent hands on a member of the royal family? On the kind old king's son and heir? It went against all her training. Not to mention her loyalty to the late monarch.

The queen dropped her hand, but not her stare. "Captain—Olivia—you care for my son, don't you? You were practically raised together, after all."

That much was true, even though she'd never had much use for the prince. He'd been a whiny crybaby whom she'd called Rupie when they were children. "Of course, Majesty."

"And you wouldn't want to see him lose the throne."

"Surely it wouldn't come to that!"

The queen put her hands together and nodded, appearing pious and sincere. "It could and it will. The law of the land decrees it. If Ruprecht is not crowned in two weeks, the title passes to one of his cousins from a faraway kingdom. The new king would likely bring his entire court here, dismissing this one."

The queen didn't have to say it, her threat hung in the air. If Ruprecht lost the crown, and a new ruler arrived, the Vanderbroooks—Olivia's parents and siblings—would lose their positions as favored courtiers, friends of the royal family. Marriage prospects would disappear, as would her brother Basil's chance to study enough to become a wise man or royal advisor.

The Vanderbrooks could become destitute.

"I understand, Your Majesty," she said, meaning it.

"You'll bring him back by any means necessary?"

She hesitated, then nodded once. "I will do as you command."

The queen smiled beneficently. "Ahh, good. I expect you to be off immediately." But before she swept away, she added, "Oh, and Captain, I assume I needn't warn you not to be swayed from your duty by my son? He is a very handsome man."

"Never," she swore, hearing her own vehemence. She'd seen the prince traipse through the tulips one too many times when they were young to ever think of him as anything but a silly boy.

The queen lifted a haughty brow. "Indeed?"

Knowing the queen's vanity about her son's looks, she added, "I simply mean, my training allows for no thought of such things. Those interests have long been driven out of me."

That was true. She'd made her choice when she'd turned twenty. Celibacy and devotion to duty had ruled her life for eight years, even if others in her troop weren't as rigid about their vows.

Not Olivia. No man had ever tempted her to stray.

And she doubted she ever would. But if she ever *were* tempted, it certainly wouldn't be by a silly fop like the prince.

CONSIDERING HE PLAYED LEAD guitar and was the front-man singer for a popular weekend rock band, Rafe Cabot had heard more than his fair share of pickup lines. Women had told him they wanted to polish his long, hard microphone. Or asked him to pluck their strings. They'd offered to let him practice his licks on their thighs. And he had been told more times than he could count that he and some female could make beautiful music together.

Snooty legal types who wouldn't give him the time of day if they saw him at his regular job as a carpenter threw their panties on stage when he sang. Old and young, single and married, they did crazy stuff to get the attention of a man they saw as hot and easy.

Being hot was part of the rocker mystique. No matter what a guy looked like, if he had a guitar, chicks went for him. That would explain why elderly grandpas from big-name groups still got panties—thongs, not Depends—thrown at them, too.

Being easy, though, he wouldn't cop to. Been there, done that, had his fun and now it was over. When the show ended, he would go home to sleep—alone—focused on the carpentry jobs he had lined up for next week, not the sex he could be getting over the weekend.

Still, the come-ons were part of the gig. He knew it, every band member knew it. A couple of the guys were young enough to hit whatever got pitched to them, but Rafe was far enough along that he never even picked up the bat. No harm, no foul.

Thing was, lately, he'd been getting pitches from some unusual sources. Really unusual. In the one way Rafe definitely didn't swing.

"Oooh, a group of hot ones just sat down at the far right table," said Adam, their bass player, who was peering out from the back room of the popular club. Snickering, he added, "Of course, they're dudes. Anyone wanna bet who they came to see?"

Their drummer, Jeremy, piped in. "Watch what you use to wipe the sweat off your face tonight, Rafe. You might get a pair of boxers tossed at ya instead of silk panties."

"Screw you guys."

The others laughed, knowing Rafe had been worrying about his new fan base. Lately, it seemed like his most enthusiastic groupies came with very different equipment in their pants.

He was no homophobe. He'd lived in San Francisco, for God's sake. Hell, he'd voted against Prop 8.

But…seriously? This was getting ridiculous. Somehow, he had become the flavor-of-the-month for the type of clientele who usually hung out in bars where guys danced with guys.

Gig after gig, the audience grew a bit more mixed. Where they used to stand on stage and look out at a sea of estrogen, now they saw groups of men who applauded as loudly as the women. And between sets, a lot of them hit Rafe with some of the same pickup lines he'd been hearing from females all these years.

A few times, he'd been sorely tempted to hit them back.

"Gotta ask, dude, what happened?" Jeremy asked. "When did you become gay-bait? Is there something you're not telling us?"

"Screw you twice," he muttered.

"It's been a long time since we've seen you with a woman. If you've switched sides…"

"I haven't," Rafe snarled. "Just because I don't pick up a different woman after every show doesn't mean I've stopped liking them." Forcing his annoyance away, he said, "I think I have a look-alike somewhere in the city. These guys have been calling me by the wrong name. Ralphie, Roofie, something like that."

"Sounds a lot like Rafe to me," Jeremy said.

"I'm telling you, it's all some big screw-up."

One he wanted to rectify ASAP. Whoever this guy was, he must look a *lot* like him. Rafe heard his name at almost every show.

"You ready?" the club manager asked. "Line's out the door!"

Adam smiled broadly. "Would you say the crowd has more X chromosomes or Y?"

Rafe glared at his friend. "One more crack and I'm gone."

Chuckling, the other man held up a hand, palm out. "Sorry."

Determined to ignore everything but the music, Rafe returned to the stage. Applause washed over him, the heat of the lights melting his irritation. Hitting the strings hard, he pounded out his troubles in an edgy rhythm, losing himself in the beat. He kept looking over the heads of the audience, not making eye contact.

At least, until his eyes landed on *her.*

The blonde stood by the bar, her back ramrod straight. Looking neither left nor right, she concentrated strictly on the stage, so intently focused, she didn't even seem to be on the same planet as the noisy crowd that surrounded her.

Actually, that wasn't quite true. She wasn't looking at the stage. The woman was concentrating solely on *him.*

Every time he glanced her way, he found her staring at him. But not the way most women stared. This one was not wearing anything that could be described as a come-and-get-me smile. The expression on her beautiful face would more correctly be described as give-me-what-I-want-or-I'll-hurt-you.

Despite her scowl, some straight men in the place gave it a shot, anyway. Three or four had approached her. Whatever she said to them made them scurry away, thoroughly intimidated.

Rafe, however, didn't feel intimidated. In fact, for the first time in his adult life, he felt on the verge of getting a hard-on in the middle of a performance.

Because, hot damn, she was amazing.

"Dude, check out Xena the warrior princess in the back," muttered Adam when they finished the song.

"Way ahead of ya," Rafe admitted.

Adam had nailed it. Other than being blond-haired instead of brunette, the stranger had that whole bad-ass persona down to a T. And it wasn't just the attitude. She was dressed exactly like the woman who'd starred in every one of his teenage Lucy Lawless fantasies.

Along with all that attitude, she wore black leather, top to bottom. Though, to be honest, there wasn't a whole lot covering the top. Or the bottom.

People in San Francisco were always a little out there in their dress, but this woman could start a new fashion trend. If the women in town thought they could look as hot as *her,* they'd be getting their own leather halter tops and short, matching skirts.

Her flat, knee-length boots laced all the way up the front, hugging slim legs. Personally, he'd prefer them to be spike-heeled, but that was his only complaint.

With the clothes, her long blond hair hanging well past her shoulders—a gold headband resting on top of it—and that gleam of danger in her eyes, she was impossible to ignore. Every man and woman in the bar, gay or straight, had checked her out.

"Dibs," Adam said.

"Forget it." Rafe met the blonde's stare again. "In case you haven't noticed, I'm the one she's interested in."

"Aww, come on, you can have your pick from all those other tables." The way Adam wagged his eyebrows said he was talking about certain tables. The ones filled with guys.

"She's mine," he snapped as he plunged into the next tune.

Rafe didn't know why he was suddenly ready to jump back into the easy-sex game he had long since left behind him. Maybe because the band members' joshing had gotten under his skin? Or because he was starting to worry he was doing something to attract the male attention he'd been getting?

Nah. It was her. Just her. It had been a long time since he'd looked across a crowded room and seen a woman who stole his breath. She not only did that, she practically stopped his heart.

He suspected she could start it again with a single touch.

Working two jobs, Rafe didn't have much time for relationships. His last one, with a sad divorcée who'd hired him to renovate her kitchen and kept him on to heal her broken heart, had ended in a major dumping. He'd been the dumpee. She'd decided her attorney was a better prospect than her carpenter.

Same old story. He was a sucker for a woman in need and had gotten involved even when he'd known it was a bad idea.

Rafe had tried to avoid doing that again by sleeping with a different groupie every weekend. But, feeling too much like a user, he couldn't continue. Sharing a night of sex and nothing else was fine for some women—but not others. Problem was, he could never be absolutely certain which type was trying to pick him up.

He just didn't like hurting anyone. Maybe because of his own protective tendencies toward women—starting with the one who'd raised him, alone, after his father had walked out. So he'd decided to steer clear of any kind of entanglements, sexual or emotional, and focus on work and the band for a while.

He'd done okay with that. Until tonight. Until *her.*

Throughout the evening, he continued to steal glances at the blonde. Judging by the full glasses on the bar, she had fulfilled the two drink minimum—or, more likely, some hopeful guy had fulfilled it for her—but hadn't touched either one. She wasn't drinking, wasn't talking, wasn't dancing, wasn't smiling.

All she did was watch. And she only watched him.

Finally, near the end of the night, he glanced over and saw she was on the move. She made her way through the crowd; a tap on a shoulder or a word and people melted out of her way. She would have no problem getting up to the small stage, and he'd take anything she might like to throw at him. Including herself.

But, he suddenly realized, she wasn't coming toward the stage. Instead, she was heading for the door. And without a single look back in his direction, she walked right out of it.

"Dude, harsh," Adam said as they segued into one last song.

Harsh indeed. Talk about misreading a woman. He'd apparently been way off base, seeing attraction when it hadn't been there.

After they finished the song, Adam said, "Don't feel bad. She probably wasn't that hot up close, anyway."

Not hot? The woman should come with a Fire Hazard sign around her neck and a smoke alarm taped to her thigh.

One long, luscious thigh.

He'd wanted her. She'd left. And the night suddenly seemed a whole lot emptier. "Do me a favor," Rafe said as the crowd swooped in. "Let me get outta here. I'm not up for this tonight."

Despite his joking and smart-ass attitude, Adam was a good friend and he knew when Rafe had reached his limit. Waving, he said, "Go on. We'll pack up your stuff and get it into the van."

Normally, Rafe wouldn't have left without his Fender, but he just had to go. He couldn't deal with dudes coming on to him, not now, after he'd been desperately interested in a woman and she had walked away without as much as a hello.

Making his way out, he heard his bandmates covering for him, giving him a chance to leave without having somebody go outside to cut him off. Mentally thanking them, he stepped into the San Francisco night, breathing deeply of the cool air—salty, a little grimy. Still, even a back alley with a Dumpster smelled better than the hot, sweaty club filled with wall-to-wall people and the reek of spilled beer.

Sidestepping around Adam's van, he turned to walk home. Rafe lived downtown, in a converted loft, which he'd bought as a cheap ruin and spent two years renovating. He'd walked these streets at night a hundred times, without ever feeling a hint of worry.

But now, for some reason, the hairs on the back of his neck stood up. He slowed, glancing from side to side, certain he wasn't alone, though he couldn't define why. Maybe a sound, a movement through the air; something had put him on alert.

With reason.

Without warning, a shape came at him from the darkness. He lifted a hand to defend himself but the figure moved like black lightning, shoving him against the brick wall of the building and pinning him there with a forearm across his throat.

Shocked, Rafe tried to struggle, but immediately stopped when he heard a voice. A female voice. A sexy female voice.

"Okay, handsome," she said, "fun's over. You're mine."

2

OLIVIA HADN'T PLANNED to physically accost the prince. After arriving in this loud, noxious city and tracking him down, using a miniature portrait someone had finally recognized, she had intended merely to talk to him. Reminding him of what he stood to lose should have been enough to convince him to return with her.

The prince might be lazy, vain and a bit silly, but he'd never seemed entirely stupid. As little as he might like his mother, or the responsibilities that came with a royal title, he most definitely liked the perks. Good clothes, good wine, gold by the barrel. No bedbugs or lice to worry about, front-row seats to any show playing at the palace. Oh, and a few palaces.

Not a bad life if you were into that sort of thing.

So she'd been certain she could talk him into returning, and had walked into that public house to do just that.

But the Ruprecht she'd seen up on that stage—the one she currently had pinned to a wall—was nothing like the callow boy she remembered from her childhood. Nor was he much like the prince she'd last seen riding his golden carriage through the countryside two years ago. Absolutely nothing.

"Well, that's one way to say hello. But offering me a beer would probably have worked, too," he said, his voice throaty, deep. Not like she remembered, either. "I thought you'd left."

"I was waiting for you."

"Lucky me," he said, his wide smile brightened by moonlight.

She stared at him. "You're different."

"Than what?"

"Just different."

But it was him, of course. She recognized him easily. The light brown hair, the dark, piercing eyes, the square jaw and sculpted cheeks. He had always been handsome, and that hadn't changed. The fact that his hair was longer now, and his jaw slightly grizzled, didn't diminish from his looks at all.

In fact, to be honest, they added to it. Because the last time she'd set eyes on Ruprecht, she'd seen the same pretty boy who'd once threatened to have her drawn and quartered because she'd dared to splash mud on his new velvet pantaloons.

Now, she saw a man. A self-confident, powerful man, capable of getting dirty all on his own. In any number of ways.

"So, tell me, does this warrior-woman thing work with all the guys? Do you usually get what you're after?"

"I always get what I'm after," she said, her eyes narrowed, her tone carrying an edge as sharp as the blade on her sword.

"I think I can see why. It's pretty hot."

His voice contained laughter and his easy manner threw her off balance. Much about him threw her off balance and had since the moment she'd set eyes on him tonight. She'd been shocked at first, trapped in the middle of that odiferous crowd, watching him onstage, performing like a common minstrel. Her proud prince.

Strangely, though, he hadn't looked at all the buffoon, hadn't sounded like the whiny, petulant boy she knew. In fact, his throaty voice had been quite melodious. Even if she'd found the music unsettling. The raw, powerful beat had reverberated deep inside her, leaving her restless, confused.

She hadn't liked it. That was why she'd left, deciding to wait for him outside.

"Where did you learn to do that?" she asked.

"Do what?"

"Play that music?"

"I picked it up pretty easily once I started to study. Just a natural, I guess. Did you like it?"

She shook her head slowly, answering honestly though she knew it would probably anger him. "Not really."

"Gee, thanks." He sounded amused, not offended.

Strange. So strange. Not just his mood, but everything about him. She'd known this man since childhood, and yet, for the first time, she began to see why other women might find him appealing. All the females in the public house had been talking about him—his handsome face, raspy voice, thick hair and rock-hard form.

That's what had really thrown her. Ruprecht had always been soft. Pampered and cosseted. She didn't know if he had ever lifted a hand to comb his own hair.

But now. Oh, pressed up against him as she was now, she had to acknowledge he most definitely was not soft anymore. Not anywhere. Those were thick, rippling muscles in the legs tangled with hers. And his tight, black shirt bulged over an impressively broad chest and strong arms.

She could still take him in hand-to-hand combat, of course. Easily. Probably with one arm lashed behind her back.

But he might actually make it interesting now.

"So, uh, you gonna let me go, hotshot?" he asked, relaxed, not trying to free himself. After all, she reminded herself, he'd never learned to fight; never had to, not when people like Olivia were ready to lay down their lives to protect him.

Maybe with both arms lashed behind my back.

"Can I trust you not to try to escape me?"

He laughed softly. "Oh, I'm not going anywhere. You wanted my attention, you most definitely got it."

She slowly lowered her arm, reminding herself that this was still her prince. He seemed in a reasonable mood, despite his strange appearance. He'd been gone for a long time. Perhaps a few months in this place had been good for him, had toughened him up. That wasn't such a bad thing.

He lifted a hand to his throat and rubbed, wincing a bit.

Well, maybe not *toughened.*

"Did I hurt you?" God, Verona would have her head if she'd actually injured her precious darling, despite what she'd said.

"Nah. Throat's sore after the performance. I should've grabbed something to drink before I left."

Wordlessly reaching down, she retrieved her small flask, which was attached to a leather belt slung around her hips. Lifting it, she removed the lid and offered it to him.

He took it without question, raising it to his attractive mouth and tilting his head back, drinking deeply. Then he said, "Damn, that's good. What'd you do, pay a fortune for a bottle of Voss water and dump it in this?"

"I stopped to fill it at a mountain lake on the way over."

"Sure you did."

"Feel free to finish it," she offered, wondering why he acted so strangely about simply quenching his thirst. Then, remembering he had been here for a long while, she realized he must have greatly missed good Elatyria water.

Taking her up on her offer, he lifted the flask again,

draining it. Each swallow emphasized the cords of muscle in his neck; they flexed, gleaming with...

"Great Athena's ghost, you're actually sweating," she whispered, finally realizing why the back of her arm was damp.

Royalty didn't do such things. Certainly Prince Ruprecht, future King of Grand Falls, Elatyria, arbiter of good taste and the only prince in all the land who'd ever had a fairy godmother of his own, never did something as crass as breaking a sweat.

Yet, here was the proof. He was covered with a fine sheen of moisture. Not only that, a deliciously sultry aroma wafted off him, spicy and unexpected. Every inhalation she took was filled with it and, despite herself, she breathed a bit deeper.

"Sorry. It was hot under the lights," he said.

Olivia couldn't tear her gaze away from his throat, fascinated by this change in him more than any other. Sweaty, raw and muscular? *This* man? The man who'd once screamed the castle down because he'd found a golden hair in his porridge?

Unable to help it, she lifted her hand, then slid the tip of her index finger down his neck, from below his right ear to his shoulder. Slick. Hot. Powerful.

A quivery sensation rolled through her and she had the oddest desire to lick her finger, to taste the salty flavors.

God, how she loved the results physical exertion gave to a man. It was one of the only things she regretted about her decision to stay away from them. "What happened to you?" she asked, hearing the wonder in her voice. "How did you become so *hard?*"

"You'd think being attacked in a dark alley woulda cured that, wouldn't you?" Capping the flask, he added,

"But no. You've aroused my interest and it's getting more…aroused."

Olivia stared at him, puzzled by his words as well as his mood. She had expected at least token resistance. Otherwise, why wouldn't he have returned to Elatyria on his own? But he seemed completely comfortable with her arrival.

Realizing her fingertips still rested on a cord of muscle that ran from the base of his neck over his shoulder, she forced herself to drop her hand. As soon as she did, her fingers began to tingle, and she realized she wanted to touch him again, to feel that rough jaw and squeeze the rock-hard shoulders.

Impossible. That was mad, completely unlike her. She'd had no interest in touching any man since her bacchanalia, the week before she'd been inducted into the guard.

But none of them had felt like him.

She ignored the inner voice, lucky he hadn't screamed for her head for the liberty she'd already taken. Determined she wouldn't touch Ruprecht again unless she had to knock him out to take him home, she asked, "Are you ready to go?"

He lifted one brow over a gleaming eye. "Just like that?"

She nodded. "Just like that."

"You don't even want to try to pretend to play hard to get?"

"I'm not the one being got," she said, not understanding.

"True enough." He flashed another of those smiles. "Will you still respect me in the morning if I let you take me home?"

"Morning? It will take me longer than that to get you all the way there."

He shook his head. "I somehow doubt that."

As to the other part of his question, Olivia equated respect with strength of body and of mind, as well as moral fiber. Which meant, frankly, she'd never respected Ruprecht. At least not the one she'd known before. Like most men, he didn't deserve it.

This version of the prince, though? Well, the heat and power rolling off him could demand a little of her respect. She was big enough to concede she might need to leave one hand untethered.

"I won't think less of you," she finally said, knowing better than to tell a royal what she was really thinking.

"Okay, then." As he spoke, he reached up and touched a strand of her hair, smoothing it back, letting his finger-tips brush across her cheek.

Olivia remained stiff, shocked that he would do such a thing, reach out and touch her so casually. The stroke was deliberate, sweet. Nobody had touched her hair like that since she was a child, and an hour ago, she would have sworn that if anyone had tried, they'd have lost a few fingers.

Now? Something deep inside her didn't mind so much.

"You've really caught me. I never do this," he said.

"Do what?"

"What we're about to do. I was that guy once, but I haven't been for a long time. Yet here I am, ready to walk away with you, damn the consequences."

"Oh, I know you're not who you used to be," she insisted. "Though, I must admit, I thought you would prove more resistant."

"Hey, you said you'd still respect me in the morning." He lifted his other hand, resting it on her bare shoulder, running his fingers across her skin as if noting its texture.

This connection, possessive and deliberate, shocked her more than the first. Especially because something deep inside her—a molten core of nearly forgotten femininity—reacted. Her first impulse wasn't to throw the hand off and flip him onto his back for his temerity, but to curl even closer.

What is going on?

She didn't understand. This was Ruprecht, the bane of her childhood, the weakest man she'd ever known. How could he be affecting her in such a way? Not even the most powerful warriors of Elatyria had ever elicited from her much more than a hint of interest for the way they could fell a sky-high beanstalk with one blow. Yet his touch had put a quiver in her center.

There was something wrong with the air here. Or perhaps with the food—she shouldn't have sunk her teeth into that sweet, round confection with the hole in the center. It had addled her mind.

"You don't mind me not resisting, do you?" he asked. Then, leaning even closer, until his lips actually brushed her temple, he added, "Because I admit, I find you irresistible." As if he couldn't help himself, he moved his mouth down, pressing faint kisses on her cheek, inching close to her mouth.

Shocked, Olivia couldn't speak. She told herself it was merely surprise, but wasn't sure *why* she didn't pull away to remind him of his position—and hers. Instead, she stood there, stiff, unsure, even as he pressed that warm mouth against her own. She sucked in a surprised breath, parting her lips, and he took advantage. His tongue stole inside, languorously gliding against hers.

Olivia hadn't been kissed in nearly a decade. Nor was she sure she'd *ever* been kissed like this. Warm and wet and deep.

Certainly no kiss had ever made her feel so…tingly. Right down to her feet. Warmth and heady pleasure stole through her, the connection of their lips seeming to touch her in so many other places. Mysterious places. Feminine places unused for many years.

She didn't quite know what to do. So she simply let him taste her, fill her mouth with his flavor, wondering how it could possibly grow more pleasurable just because he lifted his hands to her face and cupped her cheeks.

"Relax," he whispered. "Easy."

She couldn't do that, no matter how much she liked the sensations. Her entire body remained unyielding, the feelings too unusual, too unexpected to allow for anything like relaxation.

Finally, he ended the kiss and stared down at her, appearing a little disappointed. "Sorry. It isn't the place. I'm sure you weren't expecting that here."

Almost shaking, Olivia sucked in a deep breath, regretting it when her lungs were filled with every masculine bit of him, which awakened her senses even more. Swallowing hard, she said, "No, I wasn't expecting that." Feeling unsure, she waved back and forth between them. "I wasn't expecting any of this. Your kiss, your cooperation, none of it."

"My *cooperation?*"

"No. I thought you might try to argue with me. I came here prepared to persuade you to my cause."

Or to overpower you. Now she had to wonder, who was on the verge of overpowering whom?

"Your top persuaded me," he muttered. His hot stare slid down her body and he added, "The skirt helped."

Again puzzled, she scrunched her brow. Then she realized he meant her uniform. When Ruprecht had seen his mother had sent the Captain of the Amazonian Royal Guard to fetch him, he'd realized the woman was in a dangerous mood.

Thinking of the queen, she was at last able to force herself to step away, gain some distance. Without his touch, his scent—oh, Gods, his mouth—she could think more clearly. "I understand. You saw that I came dressed for business."

He stiffened. "Business? Wait, this...you're not a professional, right?"

The man had picked up some strange language habits over here, because she was having a difficult time understanding what he meant. "A professional what?"

Shaking his head, he said, "Never mind. Just a crazy thought. A working girl wouldn't accost a john in a back alley."

"You're not a John," she said, growing ever more confused.

"Definitely not."

They stared at one another, and though Olivia still had the feeling they were talking at cross-purposes, she pushed the worry away. She needed to stop looking a gift unicorn in the mouth and accept that this mission had been easier than she'd expected.

Easier? Are you joking? Well, easier in one way. Much more difficult in another.

"Very well, then, shall we go? I want to have a lot of ground covered by sunrise."

One side of his mouth curled up in a grin. "All night, huh?"

"You've the strength for it? The stamina?"

"It's been a while, but I think I can manage," he replied, his tone dry. His hand came up and he touched her hair again.

Jerking away, throwing off the strange sensations caused by his touch, she snapped, "I hope so. We don't have time to waste. And I certainly don't want to have to bear your weight if you can't carry yourself."

"Is that a nice way of saying you like to be on top?"

Wondering if he was challenging her for domination before they even began their journey, she said, "I won't forget my place once we get back to the real world. Until then, I'm asking you to follow my lead and do what I say. It's for your own protection."

"Uh, who do I need protection from? You?"

"Certainly not. I would die for you."

He stiffened. For the first time since she'd grabbed him, he looked disturbed, wary. Though why, she couldn't say.

She supposed he had reason to be comfortable here, given that he appeared at least somewhat capable of defending himself. Perhaps he liked forgetting that he had enemies. But his nice new muscles wouldn't stop a giant hungry for a royal appetizer, nor would his firm legs be able to outrun a herd of angry centaurs who'd vowed to punish his mother for encroaching on their lands.

"You know as well as I do that your family's enemies would enjoy having you at their mercy, Your Majesty. You can't have forgotten that in your time away."

He suddenly bent over, coughing into his fist. Worried, Olivia dared to touch the royal person once more, pounding him on the back. "Are you all right?"

More coughing.

"Rupie, are you ill?"

Finally, he stopped and straightened. His amusement gone, his eyes no longer twinkling, he asked, "What did you call me?"

She flushed, bowing her head, put firmly back in her place, even though he'd been the one who'd kissed her a few minutes ago. "I beg your pardon, Prince Ruprecht, forgive my impertinence."

The prince started to walk away, mumbling something, then turned and stalked back, edging closer, one step at a time. She reacted by taking small steps back. This time, she was the one who ended up crowded against the brick building.

She allowed it, knowing he was more annoyed at her for reminding him of a childish nickname than he'd been when she'd pinned him by the throat. *Bad move, Captain.* Ruprecht's moods had always been terribly mercurial.

"That name you called me. Rupie."

"Again, I apologize…"

"Why'd you call me that?

"It was an awful breach of protocol, Your Majesty."

He lifted a hand and thrust it through his thick hair, so much longer than she'd ever seen it, then peered fiercely into her eyes. "Are you stoned? What are you on?"

"Stoned?" She frowned, revolted. "Stoning has been banned for centuries!"

Her response seemed to confuse him. "What is your name?"

Shocked, she shook her head. "Surely you know me, Your Majesty. We played together as children."

"Humor me."

"I am Olivia Vanderbrook, Captain of the Guard." *You've known me your whole life, you dolt!*

"Okay, Olivia. Here's the thing. I'm not Rupie."

"I should never have called you by that…"

"Shut up and let me finish. I'm not Rupie, I'm not this Rup-rick, I'm not a majesty, and I have no idea what the hell is going on." He leaned closer, crowding her even more. A frisson of excitement jolted through her as she realized he might have gained the upper hand on her physically, at least for the minute it would take her to twist him in a knot and put him on his back.

Then she stopped focusing on how close he was—how big, strong and present—and thought about his words. "What, what did you say? You…you're not…"

"No. I'm not."

Another inch closer, she could now feel the warmth of his breaths on her skin, not to mention the blazing heat of his body.

"Which means," he added in a throaty whisper, "that you need to start talking."

3

THOUGH HE WANTED ANSWERS immediately, Rafe knew they couldn't stay here in the alley. The crowd would be pouring out of the club after last call in a few minutes, and some overly amorous woman—or man, he ruefully conceded—would almost certainly interrupt. So he took her arm. "Let's get out of here."

He again noted her incredibly soft, silky skin covering sculpted muscle before she jerked it away.

"What is this madness you speak? Have you been bewitched?"

Sighing as he wondered whether this was some big, fat joke or if she was simply nutso, he said, "That crowd is going to be coming out soon. We need to go."

She glanced toward the back door, then the street.

"My place is a few blocks from here. I want you to come with me and tell me all about this Rupie guy, because you're not the first person to mistake me for him."

Rising on tiptoe, though he was only a few inches taller, she studied him, like she was looking over a horse for purchase.

He let her. Rafe's libido had been in charge for the initial part of this conversation, but his brain had finally caught up. Though his first conclusion was that this was some role-playing game, and his second that she was stark, raving mad, he'd come up with a few more. All of which he wanted to talk about.

And none of which included him getting laid tonight.

Because whether she was a prostitute or a mental patient or someone his buddies had hired to play a joke on him, the spark he'd felt from the minute he'd seen her obviously hadn't really been returned. Her total nonreaction to his kiss confirmed it.

To be honest, that disappointed him more than anything else.

"I'm going. Come with me, or don't," he snapped, turning on his heel and heading across the street.

As expected, she came, her long strides eating up the ground as she kept pace with him. They didn't speak for the few minutes it took to get to his place, but he noticed the way her eyes kept moving, constantly scanning dark corners and shadowy spaces. She was on alert, tense and coiled like a big cat on the prowl.

Hot. So hot.

Crazy. So freaking crazy.

Trying to avoid that whole idea, he focused on some of the other possible explanations as he led her up to his loft apartment. Some were better than others. Some worse.

Locking the door and gesturing for her to precede him inside, he said, "Make yourself at home."

She took one step, cautious, only going in after he'd flipped the light switch. "Ooh," she said. Looking up, her eyes widened in appreciation as she stared toward the ceiling, which was, indeed, impressive. He'd spent months uncovering the original beams and installing the soft oak planking that he'd painstakingly put into place. He'd worked almost upside down on a scaffold to get the joints straight and make the seams disappear.

"'Tis like a tree house."

"That's what I was going for," he admitted. "Took a while, but it was worth it."

"You are claiming you had something to do with this craftsmanship?" she asked, sounding accusing.

"Did every inch of it with my own two hands."

She hesitated, then, without a word, grabbed one of his hands. Lifting it, she traced a fingertip over his calluses, appearing fascinated by his rough palms and blunt fingers.

Though her skin was silky, her grip was strong, too. Just like the rest of her. She was a contradiction. Beautiful and soft, yet hard, almost ruthless. Blunt yet incomprehensible. Smart, but out of touch with reality. Or so it seemed.

There has to be an explanation.

Finally, she let him go. "I don't understand."

"That makes two of us. Let's sit down and figure it out."

She glanced at the big sectional couch dominating the large, open space that flowed directly into a small kitchen on one side, and a sleeping area on the other. Saying nothing, she walked to the center of the room and dropped to the floor. One leg tucked beneath her, the other bent, knee up, she looked ready to launch to her feet again in an instant. Primed for danger.

Or some other kind of action. He just didn't know what kind.

"Did Adam hire you? Or Jeremy? Are you a prostitute?"

"Prostitute?" Her eyes narrowed. "Do you mean a strumpet?"

"Yeah. I guess that's one way to put it."

"No, I am not," she said, sounding like she'd chewed the words up before spitting them out.

That was good. The possibility had been a slim one. He hadn't mentioned being called by that strange name—

Rupie—before tonight, so his friends couldn't have cued her to it as part of her seduction plan. Still, he liked crossing it off the list altogether. Though it probably didn't speak well of him that he considered "absolutely insane" better than "hooker."

"So what's the story? Are you an actress?" He gestured toward her clothes. "I mean, given the outfit, the mystery, the whole Amazon warrior schtick…"

"I *am* an Amazon warrior," she snapped, still sounding really ticked about his prostitute remark.

"Yeah. And I'm Humpty Dumpty."

"No, you are not," she said, serious, apparently worried he was the one who'd left a few brain cells back in the nineties. "Humpty Dumpty never existed. He was merely an allegory for the inability of an ancient king to make things right for the chicken farmers in his country. He's a fictional character, like…like George Washington, meant to impart a lesson."

"The whole cherry tree thing, huh? Ha ha."

She ignored the interruption. "You're Prince Ruprecht, heir to the throne of Grand Falls. And you've either been bewitched or injured in some manner, for you have forgotten who you are." She waved toward his hands. "Someone has stolen your memory and tricked you into doing some form of manual labor."

Ignoring all the rest of the crap, he zoned in on the most interesting part of her crazy story. "I'm a prince, huh?"

"Yes. Prince Ruprecht." She then proceeded to spell it out for him. Literally.

"From where again?"

"Great Falls."

"Is that in Europe?"

"No, it's in Elatyria."

He couldn't resist teasing her. "How's *that* one spelled?"

She huffed a little, then told him.

Rafe had never been fond of geography. But he didn't remember ever hearing the name of that place before. "Not ringing any bells."

"What do bells have to do with it? Your mother, the queen, sent me to find you and fetch you back for your coronation."

Plopping onto the couch and lifting his feet onto the coffee table, Rafe replied, "My mother's a hairdresser in Reseda."

Their eyes met, locked, hers a stormy green that said she didn't like being questioned. His probably skeptical, wondering what she was up to.

But when she didn't look away, and that frown didn't come close to fading, he thought of one way to get her to admit she had made a mistake—something he doubted she did very often. Rafe leaned forward and pulled a photo album off the bottom shelf of the table. Opening it, he pushed it across to the hot blonde who was a couple of notes short of a chord.

"See? That's my mother. That's me with her."

Olivia studied the photograph, taken two years ago when he'd gone home for Christmas. She began flipping pages, slowly at first, then quickly. Back to his childhood, then forward to now.

"I do not understand," she whispered, setting the book down.

"I guess I have a double," Rafe admitted. "Like I said, you aren't the first person who's mistaken me for him recently."

She hesitated, as if trying to take it in. "*Very* recently?"

"It started about four months ago. Just a couple of times at first, but now it's happening a lot." Sighing, he added, "Believe me, I'm not happy about it. This prince of yours, is he a little light in the loafers?"

"What are loafers?"

"Never mind," he said, wondering how long she would play this stranger-in-a-strange-land game.

She shook her head. "How is this possible?"

"They say everyone has a double somewhere in this world."

"Or in the next," she muttered, sinking down in shock. She suddenly looked more ready to fall over than leap on somebody. Pity, since he was the only somebody around.

Forget it. It was all in your head.

He'd been talking about a one-night stand and she'd been talking to another guy entirely. The whole thing had been a case of mistaken identity, he saw that now.

Well, there was one positive thing. At least she wasn't entirely crazy. Despite the prince stuff, he truly believed she *had* been looking for someone who looked like him.

She proved it by reaching into a pouch on her belt, grabbing a locket the size of a silver dollar. "See for yourself."

She handed him the locket, which was ornate and looked old. It was made of a strangely colored greenish metal he couldn't identify. Studying the picture, he saw a miniaturized image of himself. His face, his eye color, his nose, his chin. The hair was shorter, the eyes a little closer together, the lips more thin. But otherwise, this guy could be his double.

"This is your prince?"

"Yes, Prince Ruprecht," she said, a wondering note still in her voice. "And you truly are not he?"

Rafe slowly shook his head. "I definitely am not he."

She took a deep breath, still staring, her gaze roving over him from head to foot. As she looked, she visibly relaxed. Her jaw became less stiff, her back lost its ramrod straightness. Her sensual lips parted and her tongue flicked out to moisten them.

Her whole demeanor suddenly changed. It was as if she was finally looking at him and not seeing this prince guy. Why she would be happy about that, since it meant her job had just gotten harder, he didn't know. But her next words confirmed she was.

"Oh, thank Athena. Then I have not completely lost my senses."

OLIVIA COULDN'T HIDE HER relief as she realized the truth.

He wasn't Ruprecht. She hadn't been struck with a sudden, shocking interest in a man for whom she had absolutely no respect, one for whom she'd never spared a thought in the past.

She wouldn't call it lust. Or desire. She'd worked those female weaknesses out of herself, deciding to follow the true Amazon path of celibacy, though she knew of some who engaged in the occasional discreet dalliance.

But not her. Never her. So this reaction to him had truly caught her by surprise.

No matter. Whatever the cause of those strange sensations he'd invoked in her, the point remained. The man sitting across from her was not Prince Ruprecht. Not the boy she'd loathed. Not the weak-kneed prince. Not the old king's son.

She couldn't recall a moment when she'd been more relieved.

"What are you called?" she asked.

"Rafe Cabot."

"Rafe Cabot." A nice name. Different. She liked how it filled her mouth. "I apologize, Rafe. I was in error."

He shrugged, as if she hadn't attacked him in a dark thoroughfare a short time ago. "It's okay. I made a mistake, too. Thinking you meant something you obviously didn't mean."

Not understanding, she merely waited.

"So what are you going to do now?"

She glanced out the windows at the pitch-black night. The sun wouldn't rise for some time yet. Time was shaped differently here, with longer minutes, longer hours— though things apparently evened out since Elatyria had more days in its months and years. "I'll return to my campsite nearby, await the dawn, then begin again to look for the prince."

"A campsite? In the city?" His brow quirked over his incredibly attractive, gleaming eyes. "Just stay. I dragged you over here, I can at least offer you my couch for a few hours."

"Thank you, but I must return to my mission." Though she knew he was skeptical of her story—since fewer people on Earth were as aware of Elatyria's existence as her people were aware of Earth's—she explained. "Time is running out and the queen is likely growing impatient."

"The queen. Right."

"You doubt me?"

"I've got a pretty open mind," he told her. "If you say there's a country I've never heard of, with some bitchy queen who wants her son back, I'm not going to argue." Then, he asked, "What if I told you I could help you find this prince?"

"How?"

Rafe rose to his feet. She looked up at him, breathing air that felt thicker, heavier. Like she was moving through a dense fog. For here, indoors, his breadth became much more apparent.

How she'd ever taken him for the lean prince of her youth, she had no idea. Because while his face certainly resembled Ruprecht's, his strong, powerful body definitely did not.

"The people who've been mistaking me for this guy? I

suspect they usually hang out in one particular part of the city. I think this Rupie might be onstage, too."

"I doubt that," she said, wondering now how she had been foolish enough to think the arrogant prince would exert himself to entertain people he considered peasants.

"Judging by some things people have said, I get the feeling he might be performing in drag."

"What is…in drag?"

"I'll explain it tomorrow. Just trust me on this." Crossing the large room, he opened a door set into the wall, revealing a closet. He pulled out linens, then carried them over to the couch. "Get some sleep. Tomorrow, I'll help you find this prince."

Olivia rose to her feet. "But I don't understand. Despite what you say about your gaping mind…"

"Open," he interjected.

"Your *open* mind, I still have the impression you didn't believe what I told you. So why would you want to help me?"

"I don't know," he admitted. "Probably because I do believe this guy is out there, and I'd like to see for myself why people are mistaking me for him."

She had to admit it. "You're nothing like him."

"Took you long enough to notice."

Lowering her eyes, she mumbled, "I was blind."

"Forget it. Get some sleep. We'll talk in the morning, okay?"

The man was obviously trusting. He didn't know her, couldn't know how highly she valued her honor, and yet he had opened his home to her and intended to let her stay.

"You have my thanks. Please be assured I will not take advantage of your kindness," she said.

"Got it." He jerked a thumb toward another closed

door. "Guest bathroom's in there. Help yourself to what-ever you need."

Then he headed toward the back section of the living quarters, where a large screen separated the area from what appeared to be a sleeping chamber, complete with a bed sized for a king. But before he ducked behind it, he said, "Answer me one thing."

"Of course."

"Why did you seem so relieved when you finally figured it out? You seemed almost happy I'm not the guy you're looking for."

Blunt, knowing no other way to be, she said, "I was relieved to know it hadn't been Prince Ruprecht whose kiss I enjoyed."

His jaw dropped. "Wait, that was you *enjoying* a kiss?"

Offering him a brief nod, she said, "It was."

"Jeez, lady, I'd hate to see what happens to you when you come. Do you actually, I dunno, breathe a little hard?"

"Come where?"

He froze. Though he stood several feet away, she could almost feel the tension of his body. "I mean, when you climax. Have an orgasm?"

She shook her head, still not following.

"Don't tell me you don't know what an orgasm is."

She licked her lips, remaining silent.

"You don't know what that is?"

"You instructed me not to tell you."

He thrust a hand through his longish hair again, and Olivia was suddenly curious about what it felt like. Just as he'd tangled his fingers in hers, she suddenly wanted to do the same, to test the silkness, to hold him close while they tried another one of those kisses she'd obviously gotten terribly wrong, if he thought she hadn't liked it.

"What country did you say you're from? It's not one of those crazy ones where women aren't allowed to feel pleasure, is it? Because that would be a crime against nature."

"I am capable of feeling great pleasure," she said, striving to sound cool since she suspected he was making fun of her. "I take pleasure in my training and in protecting others."

He stepped closer, his stare never leaving her face. "Not that kind of pleasure."

Clearing her throat, she wondered why, as he stepped closer, she was reminded of a predator stalking its prey. Because nobody in their right mind would ever call *her* prey. "I enjoy sporting games and competitions."

Another step. His eyes seemed to grow darker, his mouth curled up on one corner.

"And…and battle."

Laughing softly, he came closer still, until only a few inches separated them. "I'm talking about pleasures of the flesh, Olivia. The pleasure a man and woman give each other with their naked bodies."

She swallowed. "You refer to sexual stimulation?"

He lifted a hand, scraping his thumb across her lip. "Yes."

Her voice shook as she replied, "'Tis the truth, I have not found much pleasure in that."

"Then somebody's been doing it wrong."

Bristling, she said, "I do nothing unless I can do it well."

Smiling gently, Rafe leaned closer and whispered, "I didn't mean you, sweetheart."

He didn't say anything more. Instead, he simply acted, covering her mouth in another of those confusing kisses. This one started hot and deep, fast, hungry. His warm tongue explored her mouth again; she suddenly desired to reciprocate. She tasted back, enjoying the intrinsic push and pull, give and take, that seemed to come naturally between them.

Unable to resist, she leaned into him, again noting the hardness of his chest and arms. And, now that she was attuned to it, she acknowledged how hard the rest of him was.

His manhood, pressing into her groin, was thick and solid; it felt hot even through his clothing. A hitchy cry got stuck in the back of her throat. She felt helpless against the urge to press harder against him, wondering at the strange sensations.

Feelings swept over her, feelings she'd never experienced before—not even at her bacchanalia when she'd tasted the fruits of the body and firmly rejected them.

This kissing, it was a powerful thing.

When he at last drew his mouth away from hers, she wanted to follow him and continue it. But Rafe kept his hands on her shoulders, holding her in place. "When's the last time you were kissed like that?"

"I've never been kissed like that."

She saw the muscles in his throat work as he asked, "Are you telling me you're a… Olivia, have you ever *been* with a man?"

The idea brought a laugh to her mouth. "Of course. I've been with many men. I've just not been kissed in such a way."

Some of the sparkle had left his eyes, and he nodded as he backed up. Olivia got the feeling she'd disappointed him, though she'd only been answering his question.

"Okay," he said, turning to walk toward his sleeping chamber. "Well, get some sleep. We'll find your prince tomorrow."

"Rafe Cabot?"

He glanced back over his shoulder. "Yes?"

"Thank you again for your kindness."

"You're welcome, Olivia. Sleep well." Then he disappeared behind that screen.

Remaining in the larger chamber, she slowly took off her belt, unsheathing the small knife at her hip.

Moving in silence, she slipped out of her clothing, down to bare skin, as always. She did it by rote, however; all her attention remained on that screen. It was effective at providing privacy—but only until he turned on a light within. Because the moment he did, the man was displayed most remarkably, his every move underscored, made larger, more…distracting.

She should have called out, warned him somehow. But her tongue had grown thick in her mouth and she felt incapable of making a sound.

Rafe began to remove his clothes, lifting the shirt away from his powerful body and tossing it down. Her fingers started that funny tingling again, as she thought about how that bare, golden skin would look, feel, taste.

But he wasn't finished. His hand moved to his middle. Olivia gulped as she watched him unfasten his denims and push them past those lean hips, kicking them away. Whatever he'd had on beneath went, too. Because when he turned slightly, and she saw his entire silhouette, she knew he was utterly, gloriously naked.

And still erect. Utterly, gloriously erect.

"Goddess give me strength," she whispered, wondering why she couldn't stop staring. Why her mouth went dry and her limbs felt weak as she saw that undeniably thick ridge of manly flesh rising from between his powerful legs. Why, she actually gasped, her hips jerking reflexively as she watched him reach down and encircle that shaft with one hand, bracing himself against his bedpost with the other.

Did he mean to…to…

"Mercy!" she yelped, forgetting to keep her voice down.

He froze, as if he'd heard her and realized at last that his actions might not be as private as he'd thought. His hand dropped; he moved to the lamp and extinguished it. "You okay?"

"Fine," she said, then realized the word had barely squeaked out of her tight throat. "I mean, I'm fine. Sleep well."

"You, too."

She heard him climb into his bed, unable to see a thing now through the dark screen. But that didn't stop the pictures in her mind, didn't prevent her imagination from visualizing what he was right now doing beneath its covers.

She'd seen the male sex before, had allowed herself to be penetrated by it. And she hadn't much cared about what she'd be missing if she gave up ever experiencing that again.

For many years, she hadn't missed it, not once.

Now? Something was happening to her. Her breath began to come in shallow gasps and she couldn't stop those tiny, helpless thrusts of her hips. The area between her thighs began to throb and she had never been as aware of her own empty core—and how much she wanted it filled—as in that single moment. She even slid her hands down her naked body, sensitive to every brush of skin on skin, wondering how his strong, rough fingers would feel instead of her own.

She'd never felt this way. Not once in her life. And she didn't know what to do about that.

Nothing. You'll do nothing except sleep, Captain.

Yes, sleep. She'd awaken tomorrow and these strange feelings would be gone. He would be merely a man, no different than any other, and she would focus on the job she had come here to do.

She wished she could do that job without his help. Considering the strange reactions he brought forth in her, she suspected it would be a good idea to get away from him.

But she needed him. He seemed certain he could assist in her search, and he knew the city far more than she ever could. She had already wasted several days and the clock was ticking as the coronation day fast approached.

Like it or not, she needed his assistance. So tomorrow, she would let the stranger help her find the prince. Then she would return to Elatyria. Never to see him again. *Never* to feel like this again.

Which was a good thing. A very good one. Even though, as sleep finally started to overtake her, she felt a brief, fleeting moment of loss.

What, she wondered, would happen if she did give in to her curiosity, her surprising want, and just took the man?

It was a shocking idea.

And one that inspired a long, wicked night of equally shocking dreams.

4

THE WARRIOR PRINCESS slept naked.

That shouldn't have surprised him. Rafe slept that way, too. But rising from his bed, pulling on some jeans and heading for the kitchen to make coffee, and *then* noticing his sexy houseguest had not a stitch on, wasn't the most relaxing way to start a day.

One of the most pleasurable, certainly. But not relaxing.

She was, without a doubt, the most perfectly shaped female he had ever seen. That black leather getup she'd worn last night hadn't covered a lot, and he'd known she had some major curves. But he hadn't anticipated how inviting the slopes of her breasts were, or the way her dark, pert nipples would look when covered by nothing but a few strands of long, blond hair.

Frozen in shock at first, he quickly pulled himself together, spun around and headed back toward his bed. But it hadn't been soon enough; he'd gotten an eyeful. Two eyes full. And the images weren't going to leave his brain for a long time. Not just of the lush curves of her breasts, but of the slim waist, the flared hips, the incredibly long legs, lean and sculpted with muscle.

Turned on her side the way she was, with her legs bent, the top one slightly forward, he hadn't been tortured with a glimpse of what he suspected would be a gorgeous tuft of curls between her thighs. But his imagination was still doing a damn fine job of pretending he had.

He couldn't go back out there, not yet. Not when his hard-on, the one he'd been forced to go to sleep with last night, had returned with a vengeance.

Moving around his room, he slammed a few drawers, trying to make noise. But he heard nothing from his houseguest. Finally, he decided to try to distract himself and make use of the time he had. Grabbing his laptop, he sat on the bed and got online.

He should have started by looking for this Rupie guy, but something about her story made him curious to learn more about Olivia Vanderbrook. So he began to search the Internet for things like her name, as well as Prince Ruprecht and Elatyria, glad she'd treated him like a kid and spelled them out.

He found nothing. Not a mention anywhere of her, or this supposedly AWOL prince, or his mother, or even his country.

"Okay, so what are you up to," he mused, glancing at the privacy screen, seeing no movement on the other side. Frankly, he was surprised the woman was still sleeping. He had expected she'd be up at dawn, ordering him to get a move on. Of course, if she had really been sleeping at some campsite, she could just be comfortable for the first time in a while.

A campsite. In the city of San Francisco. *Riiiiight.*

This couldn't be real. There had to be another explanation.

She could be some kind of in-character private detective, trying to track down this Rupie guy for a jealous boyfriend.

Or maybe she was from some the-joke's-on-you TV show. Though, to be honest, he doubted she'd be lying in the next room, naked—*oh, God, that body*—if she'd planted a camera in his place.

That left crazy. Just his luck.

"Mmm."

He heard a noise from the next room. Pausing, Rafe waited to see if she was getting up. The sound came again, soft, like a sigh. Then, again, nothing but silence.

"Come on, lady, don't make me walk out there and wake you up," he muttered.

He got no response, and decided to give her a few more minutes while he checked out the other part of her story: her missing prince.

Finding him proved a whole lot easier. Within a few minutes of searching, he found a small article on a Web site devoted to the San Francisco club scene. In it was a mention of a hot new amateur, going by the name of Prince Rupie, who appeared at a popular gay bar every Sunday during open-mic night.

"Gotcha, Your Majesty," he whispered.

The timing couldn't be better. Today was Sunday. They'd go to the bar tonight, find the guy, and he could determine once and for all who the naked woman sleeping on his sofa really was.

He suddenly heard another noise coming from the other room. This time there was no mistaking it for a sigh.

"Yes!" she said, her voice thick with sleep.

Rafe pushed his laptop away and rose, approaching the screen. Peering around it, he saw her lying on the couch, still asleep, but now flat on her back. One leg was bent, upraised, and she looked like an artist's model posing for a tasteful nude.

The pose wasn't sexual. But it was incredibly sensual.

But then the woman began to move one hand. Sliding it down her body in a long, slow caress, she touched her breast, then her flat stomach. Farther.

And things got sexual in a hurry.

When her hand reached her hip, and dipped lower until her fingers disappeared on the inside of that upraised thigh, he flinched so hard he knocked the damn screen over. Though he tried to grab it, the thing fell, clattering to the floor.

Naked warrior woman leapt up off the couch, her hair flying, her fists curling, everything else jiggling in all the right places. "Halt!"

"It's okay," he insisted, throwing a hand over his eyes, even though the image of her had already been burned onto his retinas. "Sorry I startled you, I knocked over the screen."

"Oh," she said.

She didn't make any further sound, he heard no brush of fabric that said she was yanking anything on. Still, he waited a minute, figuring she would at least grab the blanket or a sheet.

When he lowered his hand, he saw she hadn't. She had instead crossed to the front of the loft, staring out the window. The bright morning sent buckets full of sunshine cascading over her pale hair and her warm, golden body and all he could do for a minute was stare.

Olivia Vanderbrook looked as though she'd been made to wear nothing but sunlight. Such a perfect creation should never be covered, not even by hot, sexy black leather. If there had been a Garden of Eden, surely this woman's twin had once resided in it.

Twins. Back to business, remember where yours is residing!

He cleared his throat, stared up at his ceiling—it really was nice—then down at his floor, which could use some touching up. Anywhere but at *her.* "I guess we should get busy trying to find your prince."

"Yes. I can't believe I slept so long," she said, looking over her shoulder at him, completely at ease with her nakedness.

Okay, he could be cool about this, too. After all, his ass wasn't uncovered, and she was definitely easy to look at. Like a perfect work of art, impersonal, untouchable.

Problem was, he wanted to touch. A lot.

But he wouldn't. Not until he knew she wasn't fresh-from-the-Planters-jar nuts. For a minute last night, after he'd kissed her, he'd also feared he needed to stay away from her because she was sexually innocent. Her kisses—the first so stiff, the second clumsy but passionate—hinted that she hadn't had much experience.

She'd killed that worry. *I've been with* many *men.*

Yeah, and he'd been with many women over the years. Still, it wasn't something he wanted to think about, not when he'd set eyes on her across a crowded club and decided she was *his.*

So much for that. *His* woman was standing ten feet away, gloriously naked, and he could only think about how much he wished she'd put some damn clothes on.

"I actually checked online," he told her, "looking for your friend Ruprecht."

"He isn't my friend, he's my future king."

"Well, your future king sings at a gay bar on Sunday nights. We should be able to go over there this evening and find him."

"Excellent!" she said, finally leaving the window and heading back toward the sofa.

Rafe couldn't help it, he took a step back, not willing to stand there and let her get too close. If she came within inches, he'd be helpless not to touch. If she actually touched him, he'd have her back on that couch before she could say "I'm on top."

Which she probably would.

Which was just fine with him.

Distance. He took another step back.

She came within a few feet, and that was close enough to catch the warm, womanly scent of her body. Rafe held his breath, feeling his heart pound in his chest, and his cock throb against the seam of his jeans. He'd been a walking erection since the minute he'd spotted her last night. It didn't matter how much distance he put between them, he still wanted the woman like a poker player wanted a royal flush.

Unable to help himself, he asked, "What were you dreaming about right before you woke up?"

Her green eyes widened, and she sucked in a quick breath of her own. She might be totally comfortable walking around without a stitch on, but when it came to baring her thoughts, the woman was more circumspect.

"Olivia?"

"I don't remember," she said, her voice soft. She reached for her clothes, pulling on a simple pair of black underwear made of some soft, gauzy fabric.

"Are you sure?" he prodded.

Hesitating for a moment, she reached for her halter top and donned it, as well. She didn't rush—it was as if she didn't realize he was standing here trying not to drool on the floor at the sight of her. "All right," she finally admitted, "I was dreaming about you."

"Me?"

"Yes. I watched you last night, before you went to sleep. I couldn't help but see you moving behind the screen."

Oh, hell. "Then you saw what you did to me," he said, his words coming out in a throaty, hungry whisper.

"I did that?"

He nodded, wondering how this brazen woman could seem so innocent.

"I felt it when we kissed, of course," she said, "but I didn't realize it would, um, *stay*."

He shrugged, knowing if she glanced down she'd realize it was still *staying*. "Exactly how long has it been since you've been up close and personal with that part of a guy?"

She didn't have to think about it. "Over eight years."

Rafe grabbed the back of the couch. The woman hadn't had sex in eight years? "Are you joking?"

"No. I haven't been penetrated by a man since the week of my twentieth birthday."

Been penetrated by. Not *made love with*. Not even *had sex with*. There was something seriously wrong with this picture.

"Okay," he said, remembering what she'd said last night about having many men, "you were twenty when you stopped. How old were you when you started?"

"Twenty."

Rafe simply stared at her.

"It was during my bacchanalia, my first and my last. All young women wishing to enter the Amazonian Royal Guard must have knowledge of that which they are choosing to give up."

"I'm not following you."

Looking down as she fastened her low-slung belt, she explained. "I mean, sexual contact. An Amazon is not permitted to give up future relations with a man until she has experienced them, preferably more than once. Hence the bacchanalia."

Rafe gaped. "Are you saying you had an orgy?"

"What's an orgy?"

"It's a party where a bunch of people have random sex, with no feelings, no emotions. Just intercourse."

"Oh," she said, sounding relieved as she tucked a tiny knife into her belt. "Then yes, that sounds about right."

He didn't grab the couch this time, he actually sat on the back of it as he mumbled, "I got dinner at Olive Garden for my twentieth birthday. You got an orgy."

He had to think for a minute, focus on the whole picture, not just the salacious ones that filled his head. "So these *many* men you said you have been with, they were all…"

She interrupted him. "I'm with men all the time, though they aren't in the Guard, they are constantly underfoot in the villages and the castles."

Oh, jeez. She'd meant been around. Not been *with*—not sexually, anyway. He needed to keep reminding himself she took things very literally.

"Okay, let me rephrase that. Your big party, the one that made you give up sex, how many men came…er, I mean, attended?"

"Oh, hundreds."

He slid down from the back of the couch onto the seat.

She sat down, too, earnest and forthright. "Of course, they weren't all for me."

"Well, that's a relief."

"Each initiate chooses a dozen men."

"A dozen," he whispered.

"Is this a lot? More than women from around here?"

"I guess not. But they don't usually have them all at once."

Her brow scrunched in confusion. "All at once? Is that possible? Do women here have that many orifices?"

Rafe started to cough on a mouthful of air, looking around for the camera he felt sure had to be hidden somewhere. But just as he doubted a woman would lie naked in front of one, he also had to wonder if she'd admit attending an orgy and banging a dozen guys for her twentieth birthday.

"In any case, women in Elatyria do not. I used one man at a time."

Some relief, he supposed, though he found the word *used* jarring. "Twelve of them."

She looked away, fiddling with her flask, mumbling, "Not exactly." As if confessing she'd done something wrong, she said, "There were two. Well, a little more than two. Closer to three."

"Excuse me?"

"The law doesn't say an initiate must lie with all twelve men. I did my duty, tried one and didn't like it much. So I thought I'd try once more. It was equally…uninspiring."

"I get the picture. So, was one too big, one too small—" hence *a little more than two?* "—and the third just right?"

"Actually, they were all about the same size," she murmured, staring into his eyes. "And none much resembled *you.*" He sensed by the quick way she flicked her tongue over her lips that she thought that was a good thing.

The woman was killing him here, every word stabbing him in his two most vulnerable places—his heart and his groin.

She kept talking, obviously not noticing that he wanted to push her back and show her all the ways two people could give each other pleasure without the word *penetration* ever entering into it.

Olivia might think she wasn't a virgin, but he would argue it. She'd had a man inside her body, but she'd never really experienced sex. As for lovemaking? Not even close.

How cold her life must have been, never experiencing intimacy? Not real intimacy, anyway. All his protective instincts reared up and he wanted to show her all the things she'd been missing.

"By the way, the third one was most definitely not just right. In fact, I fear he was rather intimidated by me as he couldn't manage the job and I eventually fell asleep waiting for him to." With a small shrug, she added, "So, you see, more than two, less than three."

"Two and a half men," he mused. "I somehow doubt CBS would like that interpretation of their Monday night hit."

She didn't respond, not that he'd expected her to. He'd been making under-the-breath comments so he could try to pull his brain cells together to deal with what she'd revealed.

It could all be bullshit. Some country where women had a special militia and had to give up sex for life? A place where princes ran off to sing in gay clubs?

But her stare never wavered, and her tone said she, at least, believed every word she'd said. Besides, she kissed like she'd never known what a real kiss should be like. And her blunt reaction to his physical interest in her made it hard to believe she'd lie about much else.

If he believed some of it, he had to believe it all. Which included her sad description of her sex life.

He only wondered, if she was as interested in him as she seemed to be, was she still sticking to her Amazon vow of celibacy? Because if that hadn't been lust flashing in her eyes a time or two—or twenty—since they'd met, he'd give up his entire classic LP collection.

He also wondered something else. If she was so determined to stay celibate, what would he have to do to get her to change her mind?

THOUGH SHE TOLD HIM repeatedly that she'd been making her way around this great city for a few days in the clothes she had on, for some reason, Rafe insisted that she wear something else when they went to find Prince Ruprecht. They'd argued about it over a delicious breakfast—something he'd made involving eggs, cheese and an unusual spice he called chili powder. Adamant about it, he'd left her here, in his home, while he went to the market to fetch her some other clothing.

"Ridiculous," she mumbled, hoping he didn't come back bearing some sort of silly feminine dress or gaudy fripperies. They'd talked a good bit this morning, and she suspected he already knew her well enough not to do such a thing. But men were ever so thick at times.

Alone, she'd nosed around his chambers for a while, curious, as always, about the things people over here took for granted. This wasn't her first trip to this world. Since the Amazons had originally come from Earth, every initiate had to make the trek back. She hadn't found much to like before.

Now, though, it was growing on her.

One thing she really liked was the books, especially the ones she found in a box marked *Amazon*. They must surely be special, and she wondered about the warriors who had written them—Stephen King and James Patterson. Such manly names, perhaps unique to whatever tribe had survived here on Earth after her own ancestors had found the borderlands and chosen to make their home in Elatyria.

She liked a lot more, too. The enormous city seemed to energize her spirit. Everything moved faster here. The people, the language, certainly the modes of conveyance. Life itself.

She liked the color of the sky from the window. And she liked the way the city looked so sprawling from inside the top of the tall building where Rafe lived.

The thing she liked best?

Indoor plumbing.

Which was why, shortly after he'd departed, she'd done as he invited and made full use of his bathing suite. Everyone over here took things like hot showers or steamy baths-on-demand for granted. They weren't so common in Elatyria, and certainly weren't standard in the barracks where she spent her time.

"Mmm," she purred, letting the clear water cascade from the showerhead and spill over her body in hot, gushing streams. Her skin was reddened from the heat, her wet hair plastered to her face, but she savored every bit of it.

She reached for the soft-but-scratchy sponge, called a body pouf, per the package. Soaking it with perfumed soap from a bottle, she slid it all over herself. It smelled like him—Rafe. Not flowery, like a woman's soap, but warm and spicy. When she closed her eyes and let the scent blend with the steam rising off the water, she could almost imagine he was here with her, just a touch away.

She'd come to accept the fact that she wanted that touch. She wanted his hands on her, wanted more of those kisses. And she'd been wondering what it might feel like to be filled by someone whose touches she enjoyed, rather than enduring the act of intercourse in order to fulfill the requirements of her job.

She'd dreamt about it. About him, and her, and wondered what it might be like to part her legs and take him into herself.

Despite all her training, all her vows, she wondered.

Even now, lingering in the shower, she continued to think about it. The images filled her mind, and she kept her eyes closed as she bathed, enjoying a chore she usually did quickly and expediently. Now, she savored it. Her breasts tingled when she soaped them, her nipples pebbling. And between her legs, there was a strange ache. When she washed there, she found the area slick and hot, and her own fingertips brought the most interesting waves of sensation.

"Olivia?" a voice said.

Rafe. He'd returned from his errand. She glanced through the opaque, steam-covered wall of the shower, seeing his big, shadowy form standing a few feet away. "Hello."

"There is a door here, you know," he said, sounding like he was choking on every word. "You can close it for privacy."

She shrugged. "I have privacy."

"No, you don't." His voice shook as he added, "That shower is about as private as the screen was for me last night. And the show you've been putting on is a whole lot more interesting."

"The show? You mean…"

"I think you're clean," he snapped, sounding at the limits of his own control.

Fascinating. He'd obviously been standing there watching for a few moments before announcing his presence. And he'd liked seeing her touch herself. Intimately.

Just as she'd liked seeing him touch himself. Intimately.

She sucked in a breath, her heart flipping. Was he watching her with covetous eyes, the way she'd watched him? Had he been aroused, seeing her hands move across her body?

Great Athena's ghost, she'd strolled around the room bare-arse naked this morning and he'd barely even glanced at her. Nudity being such a natural thing, she hadn't thought twice about it. Only, now, she began to realize certain movements, gestures, touches, could be very arousing indeed.

Curious, she pulled the shower door handle, opening it, standing naked before him. Rafe didn't leave the room. Instead, he merely lifted a hand to his jaw and rubbed, shaking his head as if he was trying to persuade himself of something.

"So, seeing me naked like this is fine." She closed the

door again, now running her still-slick hand over her body, scraping her palm across her nipple, then lower, until she was touching that interesting spot of sensation between her legs. "But this, is…arousing to you?"

She heard his groan, saw his shape grow bigger, but didn't realize what he was going to do until he threw the door open again and stepped right into the shower closet with her. Fully clothed, down to his shoes, he didn't seem to care that the water cascaded over him.

"You are driving me completely crazy," he told her. Then he grabbed her, one big, hot hand on her hip, the other sinking into her wet hair. He pressed her back into the wall and covered her mouth with a wicked, wild kiss.

Olivia lifted her arms and curled them around his neck, tilting her head so she could invite him even deeper into her mouth. Their tongues crashed and thrusted and he tasted so good to her she wanted to drink him down.

Without warning, he moved that strong hand, sliding it down her hip. Then further around, until his fingertips brushed the wet curls covering her mound. His other released her hair, dropping in a slow glide to her breast, toying with its tip.

Olivia whimpered, feeling the strength slide out of her legs. Leaning against the wall, she could only let him do whatever he wanted to do, helpless against the pleasures battering her body.

"Open," he growled against her mouth.

She knew what he wanted, and gave it to him willingly. Lifting one leg and wrapping it around his, she arched toward his hand, wanting that intimate touch.

He slid his fingers closer, the rough pad of his thumb nearing the nub of flesh that had become so surprisingly swollen while she'd bathed.

When he finally stroked it, she almost flew out of her skin.

"Mercy," she whispered, shocked by the bolts of pleasure that simple touch wrought.

He cut off any further words by capturing her mouth in another devouring kiss. Keeping his thumb right where it was, he moved his other fingers between the soft, slick folds of her womanhood. She whimpered against his lips, needing more, crying out when he responded by sliding a finger inside her wet channel.

She jerked toward him, thrusting instinctively, as she had last night. Rafe matched each stroke of his finger with one of his tongue, until she caught the rhythm he created and met every stroke. The steam rose, the smells overwhelmed her, and heat—such incredible heat—built like molten lava inside her.

Then, suddenly, it erupted in a gush. Olivia actually screamed out. Closing her eyes, she gave herself over to the pulsing pleasure rocketing through her, from her sex down to her feet, and up to the top of her head.

Rafe held her, pressing kisses on her jaw and her temple, nibbling her earlobe. His hand was still between her legs, and he continued to stroke, gently bringing her back to her senses. Her breaths slowed, as did her heart rate, and she finally began to think she could stand on her own two feet without his help.

Not that she necessarily wanted to. Not if he continued to hold her just…like…this.

When she finally felt capable of speech, she opened her eyes and looked up at him, seeing the blazing intensity in his handsome face. "What was that?" she whispered, needing to know.

"That," he replied, "was an orgasm."

"Oh."

She thought about it. Remembered what he'd said last night, when he'd challenged her on her kissing.

Olivia suspected she'd done better this time.

And with a tiny smile, she said, "I think I did more than breathe a little hard."

5

THEY GOT TO THE CLUB at a few minutes before eight, and Rafe kept an arm around Olivia as they entered. Though conscious of a lot of stares, he wasn't sure whether they were for him—more likely given the clientele and his body double—or for her.

She did look absolutely amazing.

Then again, she always looked absolutely amazing, no matter what she was wearing. Or what she wasn't.

He shifted, uncomfortably aware of how easy it would be to get all hot and bothered again, just thinking of what had happened between them this morning.

Honestly, he didn't know how he'd stopped himself from jerking his pants open and taking her up against the wall of the shower. He'd wanted to, desperately, especially once he'd put a hand between her legs and felt how dripping hot she was.

But he'd stopped at some heavy, intimate petting, giving her what he suspected was the first orgasm of her life.

Unbelievable.

Oh, after that, he had definitely wanted to start things all over again and slide into her. But he still had a lot of questions about Olivia. And even if every single word she had ever said to him was true, there was still that pesky issue of her celibacy to deal with.

If she had been completely clearheaded, not under the influence of steam and lust and drugging kisses, and she'd asked him to make love to her, he almost certainly would have done it.

Especially if she'd used those words. *Make love.* He had the feeling the woman needed to be made love to more than anyone else he'd ever known.

For all her swagger, she had no idea what she was missing.

But she hadn't asked, and he hadn't pushed. Somehow, he'd managed to step out of that shower, stagger to his bathroom and dive into a cold one of his own.

"I feel constrained," she muttered as they followed a friendly host, who chattered as he led them on a curving gauntlet around dozens of packed tables. "This clothing is tight."

Yeah, it was. He had been close on her size but had under-estimated the fullness of her breasts and her hips. He would pay for that mistake every time he looked her way tonight.

He'd gone shopping with the intention of getting her clothes that would enable her to blend in. But he'd also known he had to get her something that would be some-what familiar, or else she'd refuse to wear it. A woman's black leather skirt had seemed a simple solution. He just hadn't counted on it fitting her like a second skin, hugging her backside like it was Super Glued on.

Nor was the soft, lightweight sweater much better. It dipped low, revealing that incredible cleavage, the fabric doing sinful things to the bare nipples thrusting against it.

He'd remembered underwear. But not a bra.

"I couldn't possibly run or climb in these things," she muttered, sounding disgruntled as she looked at her feet.

Okay, yeah. The boots had definitely been an impulse buy. They were also black, and snug against her calves, with three-inch heels that clicked like tiny shotgun blasts with every step she took across the club.

"Sorry," he admitted as they reached an empty table in the back and sat down.

"The prince will not be impressed to see me in this outfit."

"Most men would," he assured her. But thinking of the prince, whose preferences seemed pretty clear, he suspected she was right. "Why do you need to impress him anyway?"

"He must take me seriously. Queen Verona fears he doesn't wish to come back and I might be forced to…take him."

"Like you tried to take me last night?"

"He'll be easier to take," she admitted, her tone dry.

"I dunno," he said with a tiny smile, "I think you could have had me pretty easily."

Her eyes narrowed as she peered at him. "Do you mock me?"

"No, of course not!"

"Why, then, do you sometimes get that amused look and tone in your voice when we speak?"

"It's called flirting," he told her. "Which I guess you're not used to. It's a light, suggestive word game men and women play when they're getting to know each other."

Sighing deeply, she admitted, "I'm not used to a lot of things in this place." Her lips curled a bit, but she looked only at her hands, not at him, as she added, "Though I think I could come to like certain ones…like showers."

Grinning, he realized she was trying to flirt back.

"And orgasms."

His grin faded and he swallowed hard, wishing he hadn't started this.

"I also like the days here—they last longer," she said.

"Daylight savings time," he said, glad they'd moved on to less sexy things she *liked*.

"And I greatly enjoy the entertainment provided by television."

Oh, geez, had he ever noticed that. After their wild interlude in the shower, Olivia had gone back to treating him with friendly cordiality, as if he hadn't had his hand between her legs that morning. Just like a visiting buddy, she'd harassed him into sitting down and watching the idiot box with her for most of the afternoon.

Wherever this country of hers was, they obviously had never gotten reruns of *NYPD Blue*. Olivia hadn't been able to get enough of the show, seeming fascinated by the tough female cops depicted on it.

She'd been like a kid, almost bouncing in her seat, leaning forward to yell at the flat-screen, gobbling handfuls of popcorn. It was like she'd never seen a TV show before. Somehow he hadn't minded wasting an entire beautiful Sunday afternoon explaining all about the NYPD and why the good guys couldn't just shoot the bad guys dead when they caught them in the act.

Tough woman.

Tough woman who was also incredibly soft, sexy and, though she'd never want to admit it, vulnerable. Emotionally, anyway.

He'd been raised by a single mom whose outer shell had been hard as steel. Trying to prove to the world that Rafe's father's abandonment hadn't determined the course of her life, she'd never showed weakness. Yet she'd missed her ex, who'd remarried and had another family, for years. Rafe knew it. As he grew older and saw she was driven by loneliness and regret, not toughness and anger, he began to understand how hard it would be to love someone who didn't want you. Eventually, in the last few years, she had told him more than once that it was better to not even let that emotion creep into your heart if you were going to end up alone and broken.

Maybe that's why he'd never allowed himself to fall completely in love. In like, yes. In lust, oh, certainly. But love? Hadn't happened.

In that respect, he imagined he and Olivia were a lot alike. Both used to wearing a facade, not letting anyone get too close, never showing any emotion, even if they felt it.

Now, though, he suspected they both were feeling something. Desire, and maybe more. She definitely felt it, and so did he. He just didn't know what they were going to do about it.

"This place is, indeed, merry," she said, interrupting his thoughts. "Better than the one last night."

He looked around, seeing the laughing clientele, and realized she was right. Last night's performance had been at a meat market. The atmosphere here was decidedly more… "Merry?"

"Yes. As you said last night. It's a very gay club."

Closing his eyes, he shook his head, wondering yet again if she was for real.

"Here you go," a voice said. Their waiter set down two large glasses of beer, which Rafe had ordered.

Nodding her thanks, Olivia lifted one to her mouth and downed half of its contents in a long, deep gulp.

"Guess I don't have to worry about you ordering frou-frou chick drinks," Rafe said with a grin, liking that she was so earthy, without an ounce of superficiality about her. Unlike any woman he'd ever met.

"That'll be eight-fifty, unless you want to run a tab," said the waiter, watching Olivia with shock and amusement.

Rafe reached for his wallet. Before he'd pulled it out, though, Olivia dug something out of the leather bag she'd insisted on tying around her wrist, and slapped it down onto the table.

The waiter picked the coin up and stared at it, puzzled. "What's this? Some kind of Disney dollar?"

"Here," Rafe said, handing the guy a ten and taking the coin back. Once the waiter had gone, he looked at the thing himself.

It was heavy, thick and a brackish-gold. Old and well-used, the coin had passed through many hands. None, he would venture, in this country. Not even at Disneyland.

"You act as if you have never seen money," Olivia said.

"Not this type of coin, I haven't."

"You have coins here, though," she insisted with a frown. "An unpleasant little man on one of your extremely large public conveyances demanded that I provide him with something called 'exact change' which, judging by what I saw other passengers use, I took to be some type of coinage."

He slowly lowered the coin to the table, unable to do anything but stare at her, so serious, not wavering one inch from her story. So far, this whole adventure had seemed a bit nutty, but he'd always figured there was some rational explanation. Like she was from a teeny country that he'd never heard of, one that hadn't entered the Internet age. Or even that this whole thing was a big, convoluted practical joke…one that included some seriously sexy side benefits.

Rational. Logical. Something he'd get to the bottom of sooner or later.

But he had begun to wonder. She was so unusual, everything about her, from her manner to her dress, to her speech, to the descriptions of her life. Olivia sometimes seemed to be from an entirely different world.

Or century.

He'd never been a big science fiction fan, but for a

brief moment, he began to wonder about that whole time travel thing.

"Is the program about to begin?" she asked, interrupting his pensive thoughts.

Realizing the emcee had taken the stage, he replied, "Yeah. Let me know if it's Ruprecht when he comes on, okay?"

"Very well."

They fell silent, watching the first few performers. Olivia seemed fascinated by them, the brightly colored gowns, the wigs, and she clapped for one particularly good rendition of a Cher song performed by some guy calling himself Cher-ry.

"And now, one of our most popular newcomers to the San Francisco stage," said the emcee, revving up the crowd. "Please give a warm welcome to that super-sexy royal, who gets down with the crown, it's that wastrel from the castle…Prince Rupie!"

They both watched as a spotlight appeared on the center seam of the black curtain. The music started, some old torchy song, and a stockinged leg wearing a high-heeled shoe appeared in the pool of light.

"What is this?" Olivia asked, appearing confused.

"Shh," someone hissed.

Stepping out from behind the curtain as he sang the first few notes of the song, "Prince Rupie" immediately wowed the crowd. He wore a silky purple gown, glittering gold shoes and a big, dark wig. His every move was over the top and grandiose.

If people thought he looked like this guy, Rafe really needed to join a gang and get some tattoos and scars or something. Then he forced himself to remember the dude was in full makeup, and costume. He suspected the state's own intimidating governor could put on a dress and not be recognized immediately.

"I don't understand," Olivia whispered, looking at the stage. "Why is this woman calling herself Prince Rupie?"

That was when he realized she had no idea they were at a drag show. Or that all the other performers had been men, too.

"He's playing a woman," Rafe told her, keeping his voice low. "Pretending."

She didn't react at first, then her eyes grew hugely round. "Great Athena's ghost, you're saying that's a man?"

"Quiet," a voice snapped.

She turned her head and glared, her hand dropping to the sheathed knife at her hip. "Guard your tongue," she ordered.

"Whoa there, warrior woman." Rafe scooted his chair closer and put a hand over hers. "Relax. People just want to hear because they're enjoying the show. And yes, the performers are all men."

"All…you mean everyone who's gone before?"

"Uh-huh. Like Prince Ruprecht there."

"The devil you say!"

"I don't know for sure. Do you recognize him?"

She forced her attention back toward the performer. "I do not know."

"It's okay. Let's watch for a while, see if it comes to you."

Falling silent, she did as he asked, never taking her eyes off the stage. Rafe had to admit, the guy was pretty good. He got the crowd worked up with his song. But it wasn't until he finished singing and began to do a comedy schtick that he really got them rolling in the aisles.

"No," she said, her mouth hanging open. "He's… That's…"

"Prince Ruprecht?"

She shook her head. "That's Queen Verona. Only, it's not, of course, it's like a royal fool mimicking her!" Appearing bemused, she added, "And doing a good job of it."

Rupie continued to crack jokes, doing an entire routine based on this vain, awful woman. Every word he said made Rafe glad she lived far away and he would never have to meet her. And the audience ate it up, hanging on his every word, bursting into loud peals of laughter several times.

Which apparently displeased the royal guard.

Murmuring a low curse, Olivia said, "It's truly him, and they're mocking him." Her body had tensed and her chair squealed as she pushed it back from the table. "This cannot be tolerated."

He grabbed her hand again. "Don't do anything," he insisted, knowing she was about to go all warrior bad-ass because the audience was roaring with laughter. She hadn't realized they were doing it *with* her prince, not *at* him. "They love him."

She looked around the room, not believing it.

"Trust me on this. We'll go backstage and talk to him when he's finished," Rafe insisted. "Just don't do anything to upset him now. Otherwise your job convincing him to go back with you is going to be a whole lot harder."

"Very well," she said, crossing her arms on the table in front of her, and leaning over it to stare at the stage. "But as soon as this is over, we go find Ruprecht."

"All right," he murmured, trying to keep her calm.

"He'd better be in a traveling mood," she added. "And he'd better not be wearing a dress."

"I WON'T GO!"

Prince Ruprecht swept his big wig off his big head, throwing it onto a table overflowing with cosmetics, perfumes and powders, and literally stomped one high-heel-clad foot. "I won't. Do you hear me? And you can't make me, Olivia Vanderbrook!"

"I'm going to kill him," she muttered, taking a threatening step toward her prince, who'd started to whine the moment he'd seen her.

Rafe put a restraining hand on her arm and squeezed, holding her back before she did something foolish. "No, you're not."

"Fine. Get some rope." She scowled at her monarch. "I'll tie him up and drag him back."

Ruprecht darted behind a chair, clutching it tightly and glaring right back at her. "You wouldn't dare."

"I would. Your mother is frantic."

The man rolled his eyes. "She's a drama queen."

"Takes one to know one," she snapped.

"Olivia, calm down, sweetheart. Why don't we try sitting down and talking," Rafe said, moving between her and Ruprecht, as if afraid she would do violence to the man.

She wouldn't sit and talk, despite the nice term of endearment her handsome companion had uttered. She didn't have time for talk. She merely wanted to tap Ruprecht in the jaw with her fist, knock him unconscious, dump him in a bag and go.

"Who are *you?*" Ruprecht asked, finally noticing the other man in the room. When Rafe turned around, the prince gasped in surprise. He stared into a face that looked just like his own—at least, when it wasn't covered with that awful powder and paste, saying, "It's you, isn't it. You're the one people think is me!"

"Vice versa, princey," Rafe said, obviously not liking the comparison. Especially given the prince's current appearance, complete with sparkling jewels on his ears, and what looked like thick, imitation hairs that clung to his half-lowered eyelids.

"My, you are a handsome fellow." Ruprecht grinned,

amused by his own wit. "One of the handsomest I've ever seen."

"You have to come with me, Ruprecht," Olivia said, gritting her back teeth, trying to sound placating rather than bossy. "Don't you understand what's at stake?"

"Don't you?" Ruprecht asked, finally turning his attention back to Olivia. He blinked his eyes rapidly as if to prevent tears. That made one set of the silly false hairs flop halfway down to dangle in one eye.

"Oh, for Athena's sake," she groaned.

Ruprecht reached up and yanked the miniature hairpiece off. "I'm finally happy, the happiest I've ever been in my life."

She hesitated, believing him. Strange as it seemed to her, she knew this man, and she knew he meant it.

"I have friends—real ones. I love performing. I am even in the running for Amateur Drag Queen of the Year. In a few weeks' time, I will be singing in front of hundreds of people and if I win that round, and go on to the state finals, I may actually get to perform on that marvelous invention they call television!"

Olivia had to concede, that was a little impressive.

"I could even go to nationals and become renowned across this whole, great land."

Her lip curled. "For dressing up like a woman?"

"It's a respected tradition here. There are entire movies—oh, mercy, Olivia, have you seen films yet? In a theater? It's heaven!" he said, appearing rapturous. "There are classic ones starring the most brilliant performers of the age dressed up as women—like Robin Williams. And…and John Travolta."

"You really enjoy this?"

"I do." The prince's eyebrows wagged up and down and he grinned. "And I'm good, aren't I?"

A Prince of a Guy

She didn't reply. No need to add to his already swelled head. Because despite the fact that he'd shocked her, and she hadn't liked the whole concept, she had to admit, his performance had been quite entertaining.

His bottom lip pooched out. "If I go back now, and miss my chance, I'll just die."

Staring at the man, she saw he was entirely serious. He looked more passionate than she'd ever seen him.

About singing in public. To peasants. While wearing a dress. And impersonating his mother.

His mother.

"My prince, your mother sent me for your own good. If you do not return by your birthday, which is mere days away, you will lose your throne."

Ruprecht must have heard the seriousness in her voice, because he finally came out from behind the chair and lowered himself onto it. "Truly?"

"Yes. I had it from the queen's own mouth. If you are not crowned by your thirtieth birthday, your throne—and the entire kingdom—go to a distant cousin." Knowing he had always enjoyed the cushy life, she added, "You will lose everything. The wealth, the palaces, the clothes, the stables."

"My cape made of gold?"

"Midas himself couldn't keep it from your successor."

"And Lucy? My goose?"

"Along with all her golden eggs."

He nibbled his bottom lip, and she knew she was reaching him. "I understand your position. It can be difficult to do one's duty," she said. "Coming here, leaving my troop, wasn't easy for me. Yet I had no choice. You know my own family's position is precarious. They will lose everything, too, should your line fall from power. I fear for them, as the queen fears for you."

Beside her, she sensed Rafe staring, and realized she'd revealed a little too much about herself.

"I suppose," Rupurecht murmured.

"I know you are enjoying your time here," she said, keeping her voice low, calm. "But do you really want it to last forever? If you don't go back now, you will have nothing to go back to."

The prince looked at his reflection in the mirror, lit garishly by a number of round globes of light. Saying nothing, he reached for a cloth and began to wipe the cosmetics off, revealing his handsome face, bit by bit.

"I've been so happy," he whispered. "I've found out who I really am." Swallowing, he added, "I've even fallen in love."

"Oh, Rupie," she said, shaking her head sadly. The prince's romantic difficulties were stuff of legend. Everyone knew he'd spent years looking for his one true love. And while there had never been a romantic bone in Olivia's body, she suddenly did feel deep sympathy for him at this additional woe.

"Jess will never forgive me if I don't go through with the competition. One of my songs is a duet. If I don't perform, Jess won't be able to, either."

He looked so bereft, so utterly crushed, it was all she could do not to reach out and put a consoling hand on his shoulder. Ruprecht had always been a silly thing, but he'd never been a bad person. Nor, she realized now, had he ever seemed truly happy. Spoiled, petted, yes. But none of that had ever brought the kind of excitement to him that she saw right now.

His one kind, loving parent had died when he was a child. In terms of upbringing, her own family life had been much more rich than his. She'd been cherished, while he'd had to live in Verona's cold, wicked sphere.

"If only I had more time," he said, sniffing.

Olivia met his stare in the reflection, seeing Rafe's, too. He'd been silent throughout much of this conversation, though the frown on his brow said he'd heard—and didn't understand much.

Now that Ruprecht had unadorned himself, the resemblance truly was uncanny. She noted Ruprecht's thinner lips, the slightly weaker chin, but otherwise, they could be twins.

Ruprecht apparently noticed, too. He kept staring at his own reflection, then at Rafe's. Until, suddenly, his mouth fell open, as if he'd been struck by a shocking idea. He quickly snapped it shut, spun around on his chair, rose to his feet and stood nose to nose with his double.

"You could go in my place!"

Her whole body tensing, Olivia frowned at the arrogant prince, so used to controlling the lives of other people.

Rafe, on the other hand, merely started to laugh.

"I mean it," Ruprecht insisted. "I'll pay you handsomely. We look so much alike, no one would ever know."

"Yeah, right," said Rafe with a snort, not realizing the prince was entirely serious. "Not even your mother?"

"The only way she'd be certain is if she saw you didn't have my lavender birthmark on your posterior. And it would be a simple enough matter to draw it on."

Rafe glared. "Nobody's getting a purple Sharpie anywhere near my ass, pal."

Ruprecht waved away the concern. "It doesn't matter, she wouldn't ask to see it. She'll be so thrilled when you—I—return!"

"Stop it, Ruprecht," Olivia snapped. "You're being ridiculous."

"It's not ridiculous!" He turned back to Rafe. "You simply go to Grand Falls with Olivia, stand there and let them put a crown on your head, then say you're leaving on your first trip as king. Return here, go back to your life, and I'll go home a few weeks later, after Jess and I finish our competition."

"This is madness," Olivia said. "Utter madness."

"It's not. It would work. Nobody would ever know."

"I would know," she insisted. "Besides which, Rafe would never do it, not for all the gold in Elatyria."

Ruprecht stared back and forth between them, the cogs in his mind obviously ticking away. Then, a sneaky look she recognized from childhood crossed his face. "But would he do it for *you?*"

"What are you talking about?" Rafe asked, his eyes narrowed.

Olivia was too angry to speak. She grasped what Ruprecht was getting at and took back every nice thought she'd just had about the arrogant fool. "Don't even think about it."

The spoiled prince merely smiled. "I have thought about it. And I'm not going. The end. Goodbye."

"Your amphibian ancestry is revealing itself, you slimy toad," she snarled.

Rafe appeared stunned. "You're willing to lose everything?"

Ruprecht waved a hand. "My mother won't let that happen. She will have squirreled away plenty of valuables. I'll be fine." His eyes gleaming, he added, "Of course, poor Olivia and her family might not be. Isn't that too bad."

"Shut up, Ruprecht," she said, wondering how the queen would feel about her addressing the royal prince in this manner. Somehow, considering he still had lipstick on his mouth, dark shadow over one eye, and wore a glittering gown, she couldn't muster up much royal reverence.

"You heard her yourself. If my family loses the throne, her family loses, as well." Ruprecht drew a hand to his chest, his every move exaggerated. "Why, Olivia, you would lose your position, too, wouldn't you? Surely the new king would want to appoint his own Captain of the Guard. You would be put out to pasture like an old mare."

Her fingers curling into fists, she launched at him, but Rafe leapt in front of her. "Don't. I'll do it."

"You'll beat him?"

"No. I said I'd *do* it. I'll go."

Trying to dart around him, she grabbed for the prince, seeing only the bossy boy who'd once gotten her spanked because she'd told him she could defeat him in a wrestling match—and had then proved it.

"Olivia, I said I'll go!"

Ruprecht's joyful expression and clapping hands sunk in before Rafe's words did. But finally, the steam left her head and she allowed herself to acknowledge what he'd said. "Now you're the one being ridiculous."

"It's not that big a deal," he told her. "I have a passport, I'm self-employed and don't have much on my schedule. The band doesn't have a gig for next weekend." He shrugged, smiling, obviously having no clue what he would be letting himself in for if he traveled to Elatyria—a place she suspected he didn't even know existed. "I'll go, play the prince, then come home. Everybody wins."

"Including you, Olivia," Ruprecht murmured, sounding so pleased with himself she wanted to lose her evening meal all over the floor. "Not to mention your family."

Her family. Her kind parents, her sisters—so anxious to be married off to eligible bachelors. Her brother, so quiet and studious, needing the sponsorship of the royal family so he could continue his quest for an education.

She thought of them. She thought of the prince, the way he'd looked so excited about the idea of being on television, and the way his face had lit up when he mentioned being in love at last.

She also thought of the fact that taking this trip with Rafe would mean she would have more time in his company. More chances to figure out why he made her feel things no man had ever made her feel. And more time to decide what to do about them.

That, more than anything, made up her mind. It was madness, went against her training, her judgment and could get her executed.

But she was going to do it anyway.

6

_____

BY THE TIME RAFE REALIZED he had ended up in another dimension, or a weird alternate reality—some crazy crap like that—it was too late to turn around. Far too late.

"What have you gotten yourself into?" he whispered, looking back at the mysterious blue-green mountains, swathed in mist, jutting into the sky. They seemed far away, and yet he'd climbed down a path on those mountains an hour or two ago.

Time was off.

So was everything else.

Because at some point during that climb, all he knew to be true had been turned upside down and inside out.

Not literally—he wasn't standing on his head, but he might as well have been. The whole world felt different. The air tasted strange in his mouth, the colors were all wrong—trees laden with navy-blue leaves, the ground ripe with dark orange grass. The sun itself seemed to move in the wrong direction in the sky!

He'd thought for a second he was asleep, dreaming as they took a long, red-eye flight across the Atlantic. But there had been no flight. No dream. Just a drive north, then a hike up a hillside near a petrified forest, where she'd mumbled about finding a gateway. Then that strange, narrow pass that had seemed to twist and turn right into the mountain itself.

And then, out the other side. Right into this place.

It wasn't until he had refused to mount one of the horses she'd had waiting at the base of the mountain that Olivia stopped and told him exactly where she'd brought him. That explanation had silenced him for a good ten minutes. He'd been expecting a trip to Europe. Not one over the freaking rainbow.

"I still can't believe this," he muttered, unable to tear his eyes off those mountains, the "borderland" she'd called them, between her world and his.

"I know," Olivia replied as she reined in next to him. "Again, I'm sorry for not better preparing you. But I thought it would be easier to explain if I let you see for yourself."

"Yeah, uh, speaking of that, your definition of 'explain' and mine are very different." She hadn't explained much, other than to say this Elatyria somehow existed right alongside Earth.

It was the same planet, occupying the same space, at the same time. But different.

Which was impossible.

And yet…here he was.

"You'll have to ask others wiser than me to make it clear," Olivia told him with a sigh. "I've told you as much as I know."

"Yeah, I heard ya, a world within a world," he said. "Like we've fallen into a Dr. Seuss book and I'm right now sitting on a clover flower perched on an elephant's nose?"

She didn't catch the reference. "I'm sure wise men in your world—in the place they call the government—know the truth, too. They just don't tell anyone."

"I doubt that."

"You don't think they know?"

"I don't think there are any wise men in the government." Her face serious as she tried to make him understand, she said, "All I know is what *our* wise men have said. Our worlds occupy the same space, but different dimensions."

"And they share these borderlands."

She nodded. "Yes. Some of the borders are incredibly small, passable only at certain times of the month, when the moon is at its fullest." She nodded toward the mountains. "Others, like that one, are larger, more accessible. It was through a large one that my Amazon ancestors crossed over, most of them deciding to remain in Elatyria many centuries ago."

"Gotcha. And all that stuff you were talking about with Ruprecht—the goose with the golden egg, King Midas…"

She rolled her eyes. "I know, I know. Pure fiction in your world. History in mine."

History. All the fairy tales and fables, legends and myths of his life were the very fabric and foundation of hers.

"For what it's worth, that government you were talking about? It's set in Washington."

A thoughtful frown appeared on her face, then she barked a laugh. "So he's not a fictional character?"

"Uh-uh."

"What about the strong man who wears the red cape and can fly?"

"That one's fiction."

"Too bad."

Without a word, she started moving again, and he followed. He asked no more questions for a while, focused only on staying on the damn horse—he hadn't ridden one since he was seven and got thrown off a pony at a small carnival. But at least this one didn't have wings. Or a horn. Because judging by what he'd learned so far, otherworldly creatures actually did exist over here. Unicorns, dragons, giants.

Somebody slipped the wrong kind of mushroom on a pizza. You're hallucinating all of this!

But he wasn't. And he knew it. So he just kept riding.

He saw many fascinating sights during the long day of travel, eventually dropping his own veil of skepticism enough to question Olivia about this world of hers. Everything she told him hammered the point home: if this was all real, then everything she'd told him about herself, and her life, was real, too.

She was an Amazon. She had been celibate for eight years. And she'd *never* made love with a man.

That, more than anything, filled his head as he watched her slim, leather-clad form riding ahead of him, looking as one with the beautiful animal on which she rode. He could hardly think of anything else.

She'd given up one of the most delicious experiences that existed in either world without ever really tasting it.

She'd also given up everything that went with it. Love, a relationship, children, family, a home.

Something was terribly wrong with this Amazon group she took such pride in. She was too beautiful, too passionate, too smart and brave to live like that. And though she would deny to her last breath that there was anything wrong with her life, he found himself wanting to simply show her how screwed up it really was, not try to explain it, just take her there.

As she'd done with him.

"We'll stop for the night," Olivia called as she came to a stop a few yards ahead of him.

Though it hadn't seemed like they'd been riding a terribly long time, shadows had begun to cross the land. She'd warned him time was different here, shorter, and he realized evening was approaching.

"The castle is only another two hours' ride. We should rest. Get a fresh start in the morning."

She climbed off her horse, and he did the same, glad his legs weren't shaking, even if his ass was pretty numb.

"Follow me," she said, leading her horse off the trail into a thick stand of woods. These trees, at least, looked normal, though they certainly weren't anything like those in California. This was more like a dense jungle, lush and rich, with leaves so green they hurt his eyes. The colors were so much more vivid, just as the air itself, which he'd now become accustomed to, tasted so much more vibrant.

Walking behind her, he wondered if she was actually following any kind of trail, because he saw no sign of one. But Olivia seemed to know where she was going.

As they walked, a low hum began to fill his ears, growing louder the deeper they went. A few minutes later, when the hum had grown to a roar, he understood what it was. Olivia led him out of the thick forest into an enormous clearing. A huge, crystalline lake occupied the center of it, fed by a waterfall that almost seemed to stretch up into the clouds.

It was deafening. Sparkling. Magnificent.

"Grand Falls," she told him, pride evident in her raised voice. "The kingdom's namesake."

"Beautiful," he said, unable to look away for a moment, feeling as though he was looking at heaven's spigot showering fresh water to the ground.

She gave him a minute or two to gape, then said, "We must take care of the animals."

Following her instructions, Rafe unsaddled his horse, who, thankfully, had managed to avoid killing him during the ride.

That was one thing he already disliked about her world—no public transportation.

Only after their mounts were taken care of did they set

up a small camp. Along with the horses, she'd left blankets and food—some dried fruit and meat—back at that stable by the borderland.

She'd also left her sword, bow and a quiver full of arrows, which she had immediately strapped on. His California liberal side tried not to find that incredibly hot, but failed miserably.

He had been anticipating an uncomfortable night. But as he sat on the banks of the water, he had to admit the mossy ground was soft, plush. Like a mattress provided by nature itself. "I'm glad we stopped," he told her after they'd finished eating. "I needed a breather before tomorrow."

"You are still sure you want to do this?" she asked, frowning. "You don't have to, it's not too late. We can turn around and go back the way we came."

"What about your job? Your family?"

She waved an unconcerned hand. "That isn't your problem. I'll be fine, as will they. Honestly, Rafe, we can find another way." She put on one of those dark scowls that made her look a little ferocious and a lot sexy. "The closer we get to Queen Verona the more my shoulder blades come together—in anticipation of a knife between them."

"She's a queen, she can't be *that* bad."

"Tell that to Snow White's descendents."

He laughed. "Yeah, uh-huh."

"It's not funny. Legend said the poor girl became so claustrophic after the coffin incident, she ended up a paranoid old woman, and ordered all the interior walls of her castle torn down. It nearly crashed upon her head."

Seeing she was dead serious, he mumbled, "Sorry. This is gonna take me a while."

Thinking about this queen, he couldn't help wondering what would happen to Olivia if she returned to the castle without the prince. If the woman was that dangerous, what would she do to someone who failed to complete an important mission? How might she make Olivia pay for it?

He was suddenly worried about a lot more than her family, or her job. Her pretty neck, for starters.

"I'm going," he insisted. "And that's that."

Looking suspicious, she asked, "Why?"

He tried to play it cool, knowing she would refuse to take him if she thought he was doing it to protect her. "I came all this way. Might as well meet this infamous queen and get treated like royalty for a couple of days. It'll be fun."

Even if, right now, he could think of nothing more fun than lying Olivia down on this soft ground and teaching her what real pleasure was all about. Especially if there was any chance whatsoever that something bad could happen to her because of this whole misadventure.

Though the sun hung low in the sky, the air felt warm, and his thoughts made his body hotter. He couldn't help thinking how good that cool water would feel against his skin.

And there was something else that would feel good against his skin: hers.

He'd been following her lead all day, the stranger in her land now. Never a chauvinist, he'd had no problem letting Olivia set the course and the pace and even the tone of their ride.

But they weren't traveling anymore. They had stopped for the night. One last night before they'd begin the charade and he would be playing her prince and she his bodyguard, unable to publicly interact much less share an impromptu shower.

He knew how he wanted to spend this night.

He also knew Olivia was tense and aware, thinking the same thoughts. She'd eyed him several times today when she thought he didn't notice. Ever since yesterday, when he'd shown her what her body was capable of doing for her, she'd been on edge, so wanting to experience it again he could almost taste her need in the air.

She'd dragged him into her version of reality this morning. Maybe it was his turn to introduce her to his tonight.

With that in mind, Rafe began to strip off his clothes, tossing his shirt to the ground, letting the warmth of the setting sun bake into his tight muscles.

"Wh-what are you doing?" she asked, staring up at him from where she sat on the ground. Her eyes were wide, shocked, as if she hadn't walked around his apartment in nothing but her glorious hair yesterday morning.

"I thought I'd take a swim." Smiling, he began to unfasten his jeans. "That's not against the rules or anything, is it?"

"Uh, no," she replied, licking her lips, looking nervous for the first time since he'd met her.

At last he'd found the one area where she wasn't absolutely self-assured. When it came to sex, Olivia was no warrior. In fact, right now she looked a little like a tentative virgin.

A virgin wearing a black leather miniskirt and a sword strapped across her back. But a virgin nonetheless.

"Why don't you join me?" he asked, kicking out of the rest of his clothes, watching the way her mouth parted on a deep sigh as she ogled him, standing there, naked, in the last rays of sunlight.

He turned around, not wanting to give his intentions away yet. Because that look, the want in her eyes and the way her choppy breaths flowed audibly in and out of her mouth had him hardening in response. She thought she'd seen him through the screen the other night? Hell. If he had stayed put, she would have had an up-close, eye-level view of what she did to him, without as much as a touch.

Not waiting to see if she would follow, he strode to the edge of the water. It lapped against his feet, cool but not cold, and without another word, he dove in.

The liquid relief might have eased the heat on his skin. But when he finally looked back toward the shore and saw her walking into the water, wearing the same *nothing* she'd worn to bed at his place, his internal temperature shot way up.

She had been stunning then, inside, standing at the window. Now, beneath the brilliant blue sky of her homeland, she was the definition of beautiful. She literally took his breath away.

For all her ferocity, Olivia was every inch a seductive, desirable woman. From the loose, flowing blond hair, to the full, lush breasts topped with those mouthwatering, dark nipples, to the small waist, the curvy hips, and that soft womanly mound between her legs, she was every man's sexiest fantasy.

And she was coming right at him.

Following his example, she dove in completely. But the water was so clear, so sparkling, he was easily able to see her swimming beneath the surface.

He didn't know if she had her eyes open underwater. Didn't know if she was aware she was coming close—so damn close to him. He only knew that as her blond head reached his hip, her hair brushing against his thigh, need set his blood afire.

He'd intended to ease into this, to seduce her, then, afterward, dare her to say she had known what she would be forsaking with her job.

But those plans flew out the window when she slowly rose to her feet, her mouth so close to his side, it was like she kissed her way up his body as she emerged.

Her eyes were open, water dripping from her thick

lashes as she stood before him, their legs inches apart, her taut nipples brushing the hair on his chest.

He gave up all thought, all resistance. No slow seduction, no easy lovemaking.

He needed her. He was desperate to have her, to have *this*. And without a single word, he reached for her, digging his fingers into those soft hips and drawing her close.

Then he covered her mouth with his and kissed her the way he knew she needed to be kissed. The way every woman about to experience passionate lovemaking for the first time deserved to be kissed…with every ounce of wanton hunger he felt for her.

THOUGH SHE WAS HOME, on her own ground, where tradition and loyalty meant everything and she had never once veered from her avowed course, Olivia wanted this. Wanted him. Wanted the one night of heat and desire and sensation she knew he could give her.

Seeing him so hard and tall, his member swelling before her eyes as he'd turned away to enter the water, she had felt all inhibition fall away. Every part of her body had come alive and begun to tingle, hot blood sluicing through her veins, her womanly center throbbing with a need with which she had become all too familiar since she'd met him.

There was no more awkwardness. No more simple curiosity or worry. Only this moment, this night, this man. So when he kissed her, she took his tongue greedily, tilting her head so he could come ever deeper into her mouth.

Wrapping her arms around his shoulders, and her legs around his thighs, she rubbed against his firm body, shocked at the sensations battering her from all sides. His kiss was devouring, every breath shared, every gasp swallowed down and each cry of delight echoed.

One big hand remained on her bottom, firm and tight. The other he lifted to her breast, his touch more gentle, careful, even though the way he plucked her nipple between his fingers soon had her whimpering with pleasure.

"That feels remarkable," she admitted. He'd touched her there yesterday, but she'd been so focused on the *other* place she hadn't thought as much about how good the attention to her breasts felt. Now, she could think of little else.

At least, until he lifted her bottom, tilting her so that rigid shaft of heat fell directly against the core of her.

Then everything changed again. She simply didn't know what to focus on, which sensation pleased her more. "Oh, yes," she cried, jerking, rubbing up and down and taking the pressure where it felt the best.

Her body had reacted quickly again, like it had in his apartment. She knew the glide of his manhood against her was made easier by the slick, hot moisture oozing from her womanly parts. She could only imagine his penetration would be just as easy, just as smooth and good and sweet.

Unlike before. Unlike *ever.*

But he didn't penetrate her, didn't slip in and fill that empty center, as much as she wanted him to.

Funny, she had never thought of herself as an empty vessel, needing to be filled, until she had met him. Now, it was all she could do not to reach down and grab that thick member and guide it into herself.

"Not yet," he whispered, as if reading her intent.

"When?"

"Soon. I promise. Let yourself go, enjoy it. Let your body take what I want to give you."

She closed her eyes, and did as he asked. Each place he touched her sizzled and she simply couldn't imagine what intimacy could be better than the last.

Then he kissed his way down her throat, as if he would taste every inch of her skin, and she began to get an idea. Olivia wrapped her legs tighter around him, nestling his cock against her womanly lips as she fell back onto the surface of the water, floating on her back.

"You were made for this," he growled as he moved his mouth to her breast. When his tongue lapped at her nipple, she gasped at the utter perfection of it. And when he closed his mouth over it and suckled her, she actually cried out to the sky.

Twining her hands in his thick, wet hair, she held him there, loving the deep pull of his mouth. She couldn't help writhing, thrusting, wanting what she had never wanted in her entire life.

To be utterly and completely taken by a man.

She didn't notice his pushing her closer to the shore, until she realized she was no longer floating, but now lying on her back in the shallows. Rafe didn't move over her, his mouth didn't return to her breasts or her mouth. Instead he parted her thighs and kissed his way down toward them.

"You don't... You're not..."

"Hell, yes, I am," he growled as he nipped at her belly, then moved until his lips brushed her womanly curls. Unable to help it, she jerked toward him, warmed by his breaths, shocked and so excited she almost forgot to breathe.

An inch more and his soft tongue was dipping into her, lapping at the very spot where he'd touched her in the shower.

"Mercy!" she cried, amazed at both how good it felt, and by the thought that he was licking her there.

The sensations were mind-boggling. This time, it didn't take several long strokes to make those waves of pleasure burst through her; it happened almost right away.

"Oh, Rafe," she cried to the sky, gasping at the power of it—her second-ever orgasm.

He rose over her, bending to kiss her lips again, his body on top of hers. The heat of his rigid erection pressed into her thighs, and she spread them farther, instinctively, wanting it more than she'd ever wanted anything. "Now?" she asked.

He reached for one leg, lifting it over his hip as he tenderly kissed her again. "Yes."

The silky tip of his sex nestled into her and she arched up in welcome, her body somehow knowing what to do. Slowly, he eased his way in, inch by sweet hot inch.

Olivia tried to keep her eyes open, loving the flex of muscles in his neck, watching the way his mouth parted on a guttural cry as he possessed ever more of her.

But the sensations were too great. As he pushed inside, all thought was pushed out, there was only ecstasy. It grew and grew. "Yes, more," she told him, "fill me up."

He groaned in response, thrusting up with all his might until he was buried deep inside her.

It was magical. The most wonderful thing she'd ever felt in all her days.

Olivia didn't move for a second, letting herself adjust. Once her mind was clear, and she was able to think about each new feeling, she realized this was as close to complete as she had ever felt in her life.

And she'd never even known she was missing anything.

One thing she knew—this was nothing like what she'd experienced before. Absolutely nothing. Rather than wanting it to end, she only wanted it to go on and on.

"Okay?" he asked.

She nodded. "Yes. Is it…finished?"

He laughed softly, but she didn't take offense. Because

she had the feeling his laughter meant this wasn't nearly over. Which was fine with her.

"Hang on, sweetheart," he told her. "We're just getting started."

7

BY THE TIME THEY REACHED the imposing stone castle at the center of the kingdom of Grand Falls, Rafe was beginning to feel pretty damn nervous. Not to mention uncomfortable.

He was wearing one of Ruprecht's ornate cloaks—supplied by the prissy prince—and it was too tight at the neck. While trying to control his horse, and look like he knew what he was doing, he also had to keep his nose in the air. Because as villagers came out to bow and lay flowers as he passed, Olivia told him Ruprecht made it a point to never look at his subjects. What good was being a prince if he didn't even see his own people?

He so wasn't looking forward to this. What he wouldn't give to be able to turn around, go back to that waterfall and spend a month making love to Olivia Vanderbrook.

Every time he looked over at her and saw the tiny, satisfied smile on her face, he got the feeling she'd like that, too.

So what the hell were they doing heading for that enormous stone monstrosity, pretending he was some prince?

Saving her life.

It seemed incredibly far-fetched. He couldn't see any queen blaming someone else because her pain-in-the-butt son didn't want to stop playing and come home. At least not blaming her enough to kill over it.

Saving her job.

Huh. That wasn't much of an incentive, since he didn't much care for her stupid job. Not the kicking-ass part; she was well-equipped for that, from what he'd seen. But the no sex, no love, no family, no home life part. It sucked. Royally.

Saving her family, then.

Okay. There was that. Olivia seemed close to her parents and siblings, possibly because she had accepted she would never have a family of her own. They meant a lot to her, and so did their security.

Saving yourself.

That was definitely part of it. He didn't want to lose her and was saving himself from a life without her, at least for the time being. When it came right down to it, he wanted to spend as much time with her as he could. Not merely indulging in a wild, secret sexual affair, but also battering at her defenses, showing her how good an adult relationship could be. She had a lot to learn about that, and he wanted to be the one to teach her.

That wasn't his internal white knight talking; she didn't need rescuing. Yeah, he'd saved her from a life completely devoid of sexual pleasure. But she didn't need him to save her in any other way. They could go into this as equals, on the same level.

Just not from the same world.

Damn the luck.

"Are you all right?" she asked as they neared what looked like a real freaking moat, all green and slimy, probably full of creatures he'd imagined were lurking under his bed as a kid.

"Peachy."

She didn't say *we can turn around.* They both knew it was too late—they'd been spotted, his arrival had been trumpeted, and he suspected Ruprecht's nasty mother, the queen, was probably right inside the castle, waiting for him to show up, as jowly, suspicious and PMS-y as the prince had portrayed her to be.

He kinda wished he'd brought the purple Sharpie.

"You'll be fine," she insisted.

"I'm sure I will. But if this all goes south…"

"Goes where?"

"If it goes wrong," he told her, "what's the penalty for impersonating a prince? Would I get fed to a hungry dragon or something?"

"We're not living in ancient times," she told him, her voice prim. "Drawing and quartering is much more the standard."

Seeing a twinkle in her eye, he realized she was actually teasing him. Something he would never have even imagined her capable of a few days ago when they'd first met.

"Got it."

The twinkle faded and she looked serious as she said, "It would never come to that, of course. If the moment comes when I feel you are truly in danger, Rafe, I will get you out."

"I know. But let's make sure it doesn't come to that, and I play my part well." Seeing more people rushing out from their homes to bow, he asked, "Speaking of my part, is there anything else I should know? This bowing, am I expected to do that?"

The idea obviously horrified her. "Ruprecht bows to *no*body."

"Not even the queen?"

She shook her head. "You should kiss her on the cheek as you greet her, and call her Mummy."

Mummy. His own mother would whack him in the head with a spoon if he ever called her such a thing.

"Otherwise, you've met Ruprecht, just behave as he does."

His hands tightened on the reins and the horse stopped. Because behaving *as Ruprecht does* was not on his to-do list.

"What?" he growled.

"I said, just act like Ruprecht."

As if he could. "Uh, in case you didn't notice, I met him when he was in drag, impersonating his mother. You telling me that's how he acts around here?"

She nibbled her lip. "Oh, dear. I didn't consider that."

"Yeah, I thought not. What's he usually like?"

"Uh, well, he's, um, not terribly manly, I suppose."

"No kidding."

"He doesn't like to hunt or joust or things of that nature."

"Yeah, I coulda guessed he's not into NASCAR and Penthouse. What *is* he into?"

"Into?"

"What does he like to do for fun."

Please don't say other princes.

"He's a good dancer."

"Uh-huh." He loved music, but only when singing.

"He loves nice clothes and enjoys modeling his new robes."

"Gag me."

"What?"

"Never mind." Sighing deeply, he admitted, "All right, so far it's not so bad. I can work with most of this—fake an injury or something so I can't dance. And say I've decided I don't really want people watching me prance around in new clothes. But let me confirm one thing—you seemed shocked when you saw him, so can I assume he's not out of the closet?"

Because that was one impersonation he definitely could not pull off.

"Out of what closet?"

"Nobody here knows he's gay. That he likes men."

She still looked confused, having no idea what he meant. That was answer enough. Obviously Ruprecht had kept his true self secret even from the royal bodyguards. "Never mind. I got it."

Though she still looked puzzled, they began to trot again, side by side. They hadn't gone ten feet, or whatever they used to measure distance here, when Olivia jerked the reins and stopped short. Her mouth rounding into a perfect O, she stared at him.

He suspected she'd figured out what "in the closet" meant.

"You think Ruprecht has romantic feelings for a man?" she asked in a loud whisper.

"Pretty sure about it, honey. Is it that unusual here?"

"It's certainly not unheard of," she admitted, "but I never imagined it of the prince."

Honestly, Rafe had a hard time imagining anyone thinking the guy was straight.

"He's so vain. He loves being around women. So when he said he had finally fallen in love…?"

"Yeah. I'd say Jess is a dude."

He wondered how she would feel about that, sensing this Elatyria place was a little backward when it came to social issues. But when her lips suddenly curved into a huge, genuine smile, he figured Olivia wasn't too shocked.

"The queen will be furious!"

"You think?"

She continued as if he hadn't spoken. "Oh, this explains so much—like why even the most powerful fairy godmother in the land was unable to find him a love match. It all makes sense now. Poor Ruprecht! No wonder he is so anxious to stay over there where he can be who he 'really is.'"

Interesting. The hard-ass warrior sympathizing with somebody who wanted to be free to love who he wanted. He wondered if she even recognized the way she'd changed. Because, honestly, he didn't see the Olivia who'd jumped him in that alley coming to such a conclusion.

Still chuckling over the whole thing, Olivia resumed her steady trot. But as they drew ever closer to Alcatraz—er, the castle—and more people came out to greet him, her humor faded away and was replaced by obvious tension. He thought at first it was because she dreaded seeing the queen, then he realized she was on guard. Doing her job.

Protecting *him.*

Soon she was actually leaning forward in the saddle, one hand on the reins, one resting lightly on the sheathed knife at her hip. Her eyes constantly scanned the crowd, and she scowled at everyone, as if she expected someone to pull out a dagger and go all "Et tu, Bruté" on his ass.

The idea that she'd leap off the horse and fight a would-be assassin was enough to make his own good mood disappear. But he didn't really worry about it happening. Ruprecht seemed as easygoing as a bunny, as worrisome as a butterfly. Could somebody like that have any enemies? Who would possibly want to hurt him?

Judging by the smiles and flowers being tossed at him by the villagers…nobody.

"Would you relax?" he told her as he drew up beside her. Wanting her to loosen up, needing to see that brilliant smile again, he murmured, "Think about something else. Like how much you owe me."

"Owe you?"

"For doing all this," he said, waving a hand around him. "You owe me big time, Captain Vanderbrook."

She stared at him for a long moment. Then whispered, "I know, *Your Majesty*. And I will repay this debt."

He maintained an innocent, pleasant expression. "On your back, I presume."

She didn't even glance over, but he'd swear a tiny grin quirked her lips. Then, just before she urged her stallion into a gallop, she answered with a saucy comeback of her own.

"No, I'm pretty sure it'll be on yours."

BY ALL RIGHTS, Olivia should have been well pleased.

Everything had worked perfectly. In the two days since their arrival in Grand Falls, Rafe had not only fooled Queen Verona and the whole court—having them all hanging on his every word and falling over themselves to please him—but had managed to act more princely than Prince Ruprecht while doing it.

He conversed intelligently with his advisors, who commented afterward what a sensible young man the heir had become. He threw no tantrums about the food delivered from the kitchens—not even when one of his pies was delivered sans plum and with a rather obvious thumbprint, courtesy of the head cook's son.

He made sound judgments at the daily court, delighting sheep farmers by decreeing they no longer had to give a third of their fleeces to little boys who lived down the lane—a rather stupid law, nobody even remembered where that one had come from. The milkmaids loved him for lifting a heavy tax on milk bottles. And he enacted a law that no more birds were to be baked alive into pies, which had much pleased the avian-rights people. Not to mention the birds.

Everybody was happy. Everyone was excited about the coronation. All of Grand Falls was proud of their prince who had set off on his journey an overgrown boy and come back a man.

The only one who wasn't very pleased about any of this was Olivia. Oh, she was proud of him. Thrilled at how well he'd done.

But she was also jealous as hell.

Her. Olivia Vanderbrook, who'd never imagined caring for any man, was turning into a veritable shrew over someone she wasn't supposed to want, something she wasn't supposed to have.

Because there had been one more group who had noticed the change in him and come running: all the eligible maidens in the land. Princesses, merchant's daughters, cinder girls—they all heard that the new manly Ruprecht might soon be ready to choose a bride. They flocked to the castle on one pretense or another, lining up for a chance to see him.

It made her want to find a giant to beat on.

She had to give Rafe credit, he didn't seem glad about it. Yet he was unfailingly kind, always polite. Knowing him as she did, she realized he could never be cruel to one of the horny bitches trying to trap him into compromising her so he'd propose.

That was where Olivia came in. She was his bodyguard. By day, she guarded his body from those desperate virgins.

By night, she had that body all to herself.

It went against her training, and the Amazon code. But she didn't care. Her desire for him, for the pleasures they shared, had become an intoxicating drug. She didn't know how she would be able to ever sleep again when she didn't have his chest to lean upon, the beating of his heart to lull her to slumber. Nor could she imagine the time when she would lose those deep, wonderful kisses that made her toes curl up in her boots. Or go back to being the empty shell she'd been before he'd filled her.

Not just physically. He'd filled her emotionally, too. When they weren't doing pleasurable things to each other in the dark of night, they spent hours talking. About his day, about hers. His impressions of her world and how he'd change things. Her impressions of his and what she'd leave exactly the same.

She honestly could not imagine going through an entire day without seeing him, hearing his voice, feeling his touch.

The coronation was a few days away, and after it was over, he would go home. She would stay here. And life would go back to normal. Mundane, purposeless, passionless.

Empty.

"Liv!" a voice called.

Jerking her attention down a long, shadowy corridor outside the royal sleeping quarters, she saw Rafe hurrying toward her. He'd gone to visit his "mother," and she knew he'd been worrying about the appointment.

"We've gotta get out of here."

"What?"

Reaching her side, he grabbed her by the arm. He practically dragged her into the prince's room, which was draped with rich tapestries and filled with gaudy, gold-trimmed furnishings, all of which he declared suitable for something called a cathouse.

"What's wrong?"

"She's planning to marry him—*me*—off!"

The wheels immediately began churning in her brain. "Great Athena's ghost."

"And Zeus's, too," he snapped. "She told me how pleased she is that I've finally grown up, and informed me she's chosen a princess who I am to marry immediately after my coronation!"

Olivia stared at him, surprised he hadn't already stalked out of the castle and headed for the borderland. This wasn't part of the bargain. And the idea of him married to someone else…well, it was not to be imagined.

"This is madness," she said. It was so out of character, so unusual given all the machinations the queen had gone through over the years to try to tempt her son into *choosing* a bride. "She told you this? She didn't ask for your opinion?"

He thrust a hand through his hair, shorter now, since they'd trimmed it and re-outfitted him as soon as they'd arrived at the castle. She missed the longer tresses that she'd tangled her fingers in that evening at the falls.

"Yeah. It's a done deal. Finished. I have no choice. I get the crown, I get married, I get laid, she gets a grandson."

Steam rising in her head at the *I get laid* part—she'd definitely picked up some of the lingo from his world—she forced herself to think. "This makes no sense."

"Tell me about it."

"She would never…" Suddenly struck by a possibility—an awful possibility—she fell silent. Thinking.

"What?" he asked, realizing something had occurred to her.

Olivia didn't answer for a moment. Casting a quick look around the chamber, she made sure the red velvet drapes were perfectly straight, and no one was lurking behind them. Then she whispered, "She knows."

He rolled his eyes. "No way. She woulda tossed me out if she knew. Or chopped off my head." Obviously he'd gotten to know Queen Verona rather well and no longer doubted the woman's bloody streak.

"The queen adores Ruprecht and has never once, in all these years, ordered him to take a bride. She's only doing it now because she knows you're not him!"

"If you're right—a big *if*—she'd have to know it wouldn't be a legitimate marriage."

Thinking of the twisted workings of the queen's mind, she came to another awful conclusion. "She's come up with a way to hold on to the kingdom without her son. She'll get you crowned, marry you off, have you impregnate your bride, then…"

"Kill me," he muttered.

"Yes." That sounded like what the evil queen would do. "Then she'll remain dowager for another thirty years, all the while planning what she'll do to *your* son when he comes of age."

"That bitch," he said, no longer arguing it.

"Let's go." Grabbing his arm, she shoved him toward the window. It was a steep drop down into the moat, but she knew he could swim and there shouldn't be too many animals to fend off.

Though, once again, she couldn't help wishing for that nice indoor plumbing, given what the moat was used for here.

She reached the mullioned window, pushed it open and leaned out. "Come on, I'll have you home by tomorrow night, I promise."

Rafe turned around, listening intently, as if he heard voices approaching from outside the chamber.

"Hurry!" She climbed into the window well.

"What will happen to you if you help me?" he asked.

"I don't give a damn, would you come?"

"I mean it. What will happen if I disappear? Will you be blamed? She'd have to know you're in on this." He sucked in a quick breath. "Right before I left, I thought I heard her say something to one of her guards about coming to get you."

"Get over here, Rafe, we must go! If she's figured it out,

she knows I'm involved and she's going to throw me in the dungeon until well after the coronation."

And probably until after his death. If she survived that long.

But he couldn't go. "Even if you came with me…you couldn't be sure she wouldn't take revenge on your family."

Olivia stared at him, knowing his was the mind churning away now. Hoping he heard her sincerity, she said, "That's not your problem, not your worry. You tried to help all of us and the last thing I will allow is for you to be hurt because of it."

Instead of coming closer, he backed away, edging deeper into the room. "You go. I'm staying."

She leapt to the floor. "Are you mad?"

"No, I'm dead serious. If we leave together, she'll have her whole army on us and we'll never make it to the border."

He was right that the regular army would give chase. Not that she didn't think she couldn't outrun Queen Verona's pathetic army.

"Go, get the real Ruprecht, drag his ass back here, let him take the crown. Then the queen can't touch me, and she can't punish you, or anyone you care about, for helping me."

She grabbed him and pulled. "Here's a better idea. I drag *your* ass out of this place before she marries you to some simpering virgin, then cuts your heart out."

"I don't like simpering virgins," he said with a grin. "I like bad-girl ones."

"I wasn't a virgin," she reminded him.

"Yeah, babe, you were," he said, so tender, sweet. He lifted a hand to her face, cupping her cheek, twining his fingers in her hair. "Besides, the woman I'm going to spend my wedding night with has a knife strapped to her thigh. Nobody's going to get close to my heart…except her."

Olivia froze, unsure of his meaning, even though it wasn't too difficult to understand.

"This isn't the time, and it isn't the place. But I'm telling you now, Olivia Vanderbrook, when this is over, and we're free, I'm going to ask you a question."

She licked her lips, gazing into his beautiful eyes, memorizing each line and curve of his handsome face. This man was risking his life, not just for her but for her family— for those she cared about, people he'd never even met. He was willing to lay down everything not just to keep her safe, but to make her happy.

Did his world make many such men? Hers certainly didn't. She had never met a single one.

"Go," he told her. "I'll buy you as much time as I can."

She thrust her hands into his hair and tugged him close. "I'll be back for you, even if I have to slay a dragon, I will come back," she promised, then kissed him, hard, fast, deep, then added, "I swear it."

"I know."

Moving closer to the door, he backed against it to prevent anyone from entering until she'd made her escape.

She climbed back onto the ledge.

"I love you, Olivia," he told her with a simple smile that reached into her chest and twisted her heart.

And then she jumped.

8

THE DAY OF HIS CORONATION dawned bright and clear, and from within his badly decorated, stuffy room, Rafe could hear the maids singing and the guards whistling like they were all part of some movie made by Walt Disney.

Oh. And Wes Craven.

Because though it was cheerful, it was also shaping up to be pretty damn scary.

Rafe no longer had any doubt Olivia was right about Queen Verona's plans. The woman had all but admitted it, daring him to challenge her intentions for his wedding to a princess named Bumblebee or Butterfly or Bambi or something, a young woman who lived in a neighboring kingdom and had the personality of a freshly pulled turnip. He had no doubt she would be easy for Verona to control once she managed to get rid of him.

The queen hadn't gone as far as accusing him of being an imposter. But she had talked about arranging a "proof of lineage" ceremony before the coronation. All so he could show his bare, totally not birthmarked backside to a bunch of people who would immediately realize he wasn't the prince of the realm.

My kingdom for a purple Sharpie.

Rafe didn't fear that Olivia wouldn't return. Honestly, his biggest fear was that she would—alone. Ruprecht was a stubborn man. If he still didn't want to come home—even knowing it could cost Rafe his life—the prince would probably do everything he could to escape her.

She'd come anyway. Of that, he had no doubt.

And the queen would be waiting for her.

Ever since Olivia had leapt out of his window, Verona had been making ominous comments about her "unreliable" captain of the guard. Rafe had said she'd received some urgent message from home and had to leave, but the queen hadn't really bought it.

Still, she hadn't ordered Olivia's arrest. She had to fear Rafe would back out of everything if she did. But he knew it was only a matter of time. Once the crown was on his head and a ring on his finger, Olivia's name would be on a death warrant. No doubt about it.

"Are you ready, Your Majesty?" asked one of the tailors who'd made this awful, ugly coronation costume. With the amount of gold and precious jewels on the thing, it should have come from Tiffany's.

"I'm fine," he barked. "When do we have to go?"

The tailor bobbed his head, bowing. "Within the hour."

Which meant, in Earth time, about fifty minutes.

He had that long to figure out how to remain single, not to mention alive, throughout the night.

Soon enough, that hour came to an end. Two armed guards—men, not Amazons, who might be more loyal to Olivia—came to his door to escort him to the great hall, where rulers from all the kingdoms were waiting to see him take over as king of Grand Falls.

Including his so-called mother. Not to mention his so-called wife.

His head up, he walked down the long stone corridor,

GET 2 BOOKS

We'd like to send you two *Harlequin® Blaze™* novels absolutely free. Accepting them puts you under no obligation to purchase any more books.

HOW TO GET YOUR
2 FREE BOOKS AND 2 FREE GIFTS

1. Return the reply card today, and we'll send you two *Harlequin Blaze* novels, absolutely free! We'll even pay the postage!

2. Accepting free books places you under no obligation to buy anything, ever. Whatever you decide, the free books and gifts are yours to keep, free!

3. We hope that after receiving your free books you'll want to remain a subscriber, but the choice is yours—to continue or cancel, any time at all!

EXTRA BONUS

You'll also get two free mystery gifts! (worth about $10)

FREE!

▸ DETACH AND MAIL CARD TODAY! ▸

(H-B-05/10)

The Reader Service — Here's how it works:

Accepting your 2 free books and 2 free mystery gifts (mystery gifts worth approximately $10.00) places you under no obligation to buy anything. You may keep the books and gifts and return the shipping statement marked "cancel." If you do not cancel, about a month later we'll send you 6 additional books and bill you just $4.24 each in the U.S. or $4.71 each in Canada. That is a savings of at least 15% off the cover price. It's quite a bargain! Shipping and handling is just 50¢ per book.* You may cancel at any time, but if you choose to continue, every month we'll send you 6 more books, which you may either purchase at the discount price or return to us and cancel your subscription.

*Terms and prices subject to change without notice. Prices do not include applicable taxes. Sales tax applicable in N.Y. Canadian residents will be charged applicable provincial taxes and GST. Offer not valid in Quebec. Credit or debit balances in a customer's account(s) may be offset by any other outstanding balance owed by or to the customer. Books received may not be as shown.

If offer card is missing, write to The Reader Service, P.O. Box 1867, Buffalo, NY 14240-1867 or visit www.ReaderService.com

BUSINESS REPLY MAIL

FIRST-CLASS MAIL   PERMIT NO. 717   BUFFALO, NY

POSTAGE WILL BE PAID BY ADDRESSEE

THE READER SERVICE
PO BOX 1867
BUFFALO NY 14240-9952

NO POSTAGE
NECESSARY
IF MAILED
IN THE
UNITED STATES

hearing the ominous click of his fussy shoes on the floor. The two guards clomped along behind him.

But suddenly, between one stride and the next, he heard an extra tap. He strode again—heard the clomps, and another tap. Soft, nearly inaudible. He figured it was meant for his ears alone, so he could ready himself for her assault.

Rafe was smiling before he reached the junction between the private quarters and the public part of the castle.

Because they were being followed. Stalked.

"Oh, dear," he said, imitating Ruprecht as he dropped a nauseatingly scented handkerchief to the floor. He stared at it, arrogant, knowing a prince would never bend over to retrieve it for himself. Of course, one of the guards did.

Olivia leapt the moment the guy's knee hit the stone floor. Swinging on a velvet tapestry, she flew out from a side hallway, her booted feet sending the upright guard flying. She landed in a squat, swinging her leg to kick the kneeling one in the face. Her fists were as fast as her feet and in less than twenty seconds, both men were flat on their backs, unconscious.

Three seconds after that, she was in his arms.

"Rafe!" she cried, throwing herself against him. He caught her, tangling his hands in her blond hair, looking down at her beautiful, exhausted face.

"Cutting it a little close, weren't you, babe?" he asked.

She didn't answer. Instead, Prince Ruprecht, who emerged from the side corridor, did. "Sorry. I asked her to wait until we at least got to do our number for the semifinals."

We. Rafe peered past the prince, seeing an average-looking guy whose eyes were about the size of dinner plates hovering behind Ruprecht. This, he assumed, was Jess. Who looked like he feared he'd landed in Mother Goose hell.

Ruprecht, who sounded much more subdued and looked

much more regal than he had the last time Rafe had seen him, extended his hand in an Earth-like gesture of friendship. "I owe you an apology. I never dreamed my mother would sink to such depths. I would not have asked you to do this had I thought you would actually be in any danger."

Rafe shook his double's hand. "I know that."

The future king, his posture straight, his voice deep and unwavering, asked, "Are we ready, then?"

"More than," Rafe told the prince, shrugging out of the royal robes and handing them over. "You have a plan?"

Olivia answered. "Yep. First things first. Ruprecht gets the crown on his head. Once he's officially king, he gets Queen Verona alone to prove to her that he's the real deal, then breaks his engagement."

"And sends mother off to a distant castle," the prince added, "where she will live out the rest of her days under guard."

"Yep, that sounds like a plan, all right." Rafe grinned at the prince. "I would love to see the queen's face when you moon her to prove who you really are."

The prince, who'd spent a lot of time in the U.S. of A., obviously knew what he meant, because he laughed heartily. Though his laughter faded, his smile remained as he said, "I hear you've done some good things since you've been here."

He shrugged. "Common sense stuff."

"Earth common sense," Ruprecht said. "Some of which, you might be glad to know, has rubbed off."

Rafe was glad to hear that. "Just try to go easy on the dwarf union. They really did get screwed on that last mining contract."

"Done. Goodbye, Rafe Cabot."

"Goodbye, Your Majesty."

Ruprecht and Olivia exchanged a long look, then the prince and his friend walked a few paces down the corridor to give them privacy.

"You need to go," she said as soon as they were alone. "Two of my most trusted lieutenants are waiting outside with fresh horses. They'll get you to the borderland."

"Why can't I wait for you?"

"Rafe, no matter what the prince says, you and I both know Queen Verona isn't going to take this quietly. She likes this new plan of hers. She'll fight, and some who are loyal to her will help."

He tensed, not liking the thought of her going into some kind of battle.

"If you're here, she'll try to use you to discredit the prince, raise doubts about his intentions and his judgment. You have to go."

That made sense. But he didn't think it was the whole story.

"Is that all? Or are you desperate to get me out of the line of arrow-fire?"

She shrugged, a weary smile tugging at her mouth. "Well, there is that."

He stepped closer, dropping his hands to cup her waist, his fingertips stroking small circles on her back. "You know, Olivia Vanderbrook, you make it awfully hard for a guy to be your knight in shining armor."

He didn't doubt she knew what he meant. In one of their late-night conversations in his bed, he'd told her about that, admitting he'd made mistakes in his effort to save women from their own sad situations.

She'd told him the day she needed a man to save her was the day she gave up her sword for a funeral shroud.

"Don't worry about it." She wrinkled her nose. "The *real* ones—noble and chivalrous, sweeping their ladies off their feet—are all gone. Those who are left are flatulent and crass."

"Such a romantic," he said, laughing as he bent to kiss her softly, gently.

She kissed him back, sliding her arms around his neck, pressing hard against him, as if she feared letting go. But she didn't relax in his embrace, remaining tense, a little stiff.

A hint of worry began to crawl up his spine.

When the kiss ended, he said, "Okay, beautiful. Go have fun playing war." His voice light, he added, "When can I expect you to join me?"

Her eyes dropped closed.

And that's when he knew why she'd been tense.

"You're not coming," he whispered.

She shook her head.

"Ever."

Another shake, and her eyes opened again. They swam with moisture, emotion. "I can't, Rafe. My duty…"

"Is to yourself," he snapped. "Or it should be. To your own happiness. Haven't you figured that out yet?"

She licked her lips, then stepped back, her body hardening even as her voice grew soft and tremulous. "I want to be with you. Truly. But I have promised Ruprecht I would take Verona away and guard over her so she doesn't try to cause trouble. I fear she might try to incite a civil war."

"There are plenty of other soldiers in this kingdom," he said, not believing she was choosing this solitary, sad life over what they had together.

"It's a great honor to be asked," she murmured. "I will be high in the king's favor, which means…"

"That your family will be, too."

She nodded once.

He couldn't let it end like this, couldn't let her walk away. "Don't do this. Come with me, Liv."

The prince cleared his throat, and at their feet, the two guards groaned as they started to come around. Loud bells began to peal and he knew the kingdom was being called to celebrate the impending crowning of the new king.

They sounded like the bells out of Poe's nightmare. Like sadness, loss. The end.

"Don't," he urged her.

"I have no other choice," she whispered. "Goodbye, Rafe."

Then, turning her back to him, the woman he loved walked solemnly to her monarch, and led him to his coronation.

9

Ten Days Later

THE DOWNTOWN SAN FRANCISCO bar was packed.

Laughing, drinking revelers filled every table, and each bit of floor space was taken up with women in tight dresses and men trying to look down them. The exchange of drinks and smiles for meaningless sex was all but given.

A meat market.

Olivia hadn't understood that term before. Now she got it. And considering how many of the women here had been talking about the hot, sexy lead singer of the band, as if he were a juicy side of mutton and they a pack of hungry dogs, she definitely did not like it.

As she stood in the shadows, in a corner near the door, she tried to figure out what she was going to say to Rafe when they finally came face-to-face.

It probably depended on his expression. Would he be happy to see her? Would he possibly repeat those amazing words he had whispered before she'd leapt out of the castle window?

I love you.

Did he still? Could he possibly still care for her after she'd rejected him, choosing her career, her duty, her family, over what they could have together?

She'd regretted that choice as soon as she'd turned around and walked away from him. It had been all she could do not to let the prince see the tears filling the eyes of his strongest, most powerful guard.

"I'm sorry," she whispered. They would be the first words she would say. She only hoped he would want to hear the rest.

She'd been watching him for an hour, having slipped into the bar while his band performed, but staying out of sight. It had been enough to watch him for a while, drink in his familiar face while noting the slight gauntness in his cheeks and the weariness in his eyes.

He looked unwell. As if he'd been sick, or hadn't slept for a fortnight.

She understood. Their separation had been the same for her. She hadn't slept a full night since she'd let him get away.

"Last call!" the man behind the bar said, his voice rising to be heard over the song Rafe and his group had started to perform.

Time was running out. No more lurking in the shadows, waiting with the kind of uncertainty she had never, in her life, felt about anything. She took a deep breath and eased through the throng, winding her way toward the stage.

Listening to the song, she never took her eyes off the singer. As she moved, she thought about the first time she'd laid eyes on him, the way she hadn't liked his music.

Now she knew why.

It stirred her, aroused her, and she hadn't been able to deal with that before. Never having felt desire, she had been uncomfortable with the instinctive way her body had reacted to his raw, sensual performance.

Now that she understood, she realized why her heart was pounding and she felt edgy. Aware.

Rafe's raspy voice defined *sexy,* and the evocative word pictures he painted made her think wild, sensual thoughts. The hard, thrumming beat reverberated deep inside her, reminding her of the way they would lose themselves in deep, pounding passion.

Oh, she definitely liked his songs now. She thought she could listen to him sing every day for the rest of her life and always react with that primal hunger.

"Hey, watch out…" someone said as she pushed past the final few people surrounding the stage.

She ignored them, knowing immediately when Rafe spotted her. He stumbled over his words, falling silent right in the middle of a verse.

Olivia looked up at him, seeing the shock on his handsome face. Shock—but nothing more that she could identify. His eyes didn't light up with happiness, nor did he smile in greeting. And he said not a word. Instead, he simply stared down at her, hard, intensity rolling off him as the seconds dragged on and he continued to ignore everyone else in the room.

Then, without a word, he pulled his instrument—his guitar—up and off his shoulders. He shoved it to one of his surprised-looking bandmates. Olivia held her breath, not knowing if he was going to storm out without even speaking to her. It would be no more than she deserved.

She let the breath out when he hopped off the stage right in front of her. And sighed with utter happiness when, still saying nothing, Rafe lifted his hands, slid them into her hair and pulled her forward to kiss her.

Flooded with joy, Olivia threw her arms around his neck. Parting her lips, she kissed him back, deeply and hungrily. She pressed against him, soaking up the heat and power of his sweat-slicked body, inhaling his manly scent, letting herself believe he was really here and really wanted her and she was never going to be parted from him again.

Finally, he ended the kiss, but he didn't let her go, continuing to cup her face.

"What are you…"

"I'm sorry!"

They smiled as their words overlapped.

"It took me a while," she said, "but I got here."

"Have to slay any dragons along the way?"

"Not yet," she said with a shy smile. "But you never know."

He kissed her again, even deeper this time, and she began to shake, her legs trembling as desire and emotion and love and gratitude flooded her body.

"Let's get out of here," he said when they drew apart.

"Yes, please."

Without warning, he bent and swooped her off her feet, one powerful arm looped beneath her bare knees, the other curled around her back. Every place his fingers touched, her skin tingled with delight.

He carried her like a damsel, easily, as if she weighed nothing at all. For the first time in her life, Olivia felt feminine and claimed, cherished and wanted.

Glancing over his shoulder at his friends, he mouthed something. They nodded, smiling broadly at Olivia. She smiled back, thinking about this new life she'd have to get used to—meeting other people, getting to know them in this strange new place.

There were good things to explore—like television, and the movies Ruprecht had gone on about. There were also bad ones—like stoplights and exact change. Olivia felt ready to confront them with all of her warrior's heart, as long as Rafe was right there with her. Or, sometimes, carrying her.

She tightened her arms around his neck, amazed at how much she liked this. Being literally swept off her feet.

"No more knights, huh?" he whispered, laughter in his voice.

Olivia didn't reply, she merely dropped her head onto his shoulder and tucked her face against his neck.

The crowd, who'd been watching wide-eyed, parted as Rafe carried her to the door. She saw a few women frown, but most of them smiled, as if they themselves had been given renewed hope for their own prospects because of Rafe's romantic display.

It was indeed…knightly.

Once they were outside, he kept walking, not putting her down even when they left the crowded club far behind them. She recognized the street and knew they weren't far from his building. Keeping her head on his shoulder, her lips close enough to his neck to press soft kisses there, she was content to be carried like this, in silence, knowing all that needed to be said would wait until they were in the privacy of his home.

They were there in minutes. After he carried her inside and let her down to shut the door behind them, Rafe kissed her again, slower this time. That mind-numbing, toe-curling pleasure washed over her and she wanted to draw him down onto the floor to show him how sorry she was in the most elemental way possible.

But she needed to say some words first.

"I made an awful mistake," she whispered, drawing back to look up at him with every bit of sorrow she felt.

"I know," he told her, not sounding arrogant, just certain of how much he knew her. And them.

"I regretted it the minute I walked away from you. Had things not 'gone south' and had I not had to battle one of

Verona's men to the death, I would have come after you immediately, long before you could reach the border."

He sighed deeply, lifting his eyes toward the ceiling and muttering something. She suspected it had to do with that to-the-death part, though she didn't know why, since her presence here proved she wasn't the one who'd died.

"Is everything all right in your homeland?" he asked, as if wanting to get the particulars out of the way before they proceeded to the things that really mattered—like their relationship. "The prince?"

"Now king," she told him. "Fine, happy."

"Married?"

She shook her head. "Hardly. His fiancée was safely escorted home and Ruprecht has introduced the court to his closest advisor, Jess of the Californias."

A low rumble of laughter built in his chest. But it didn't emerge from his lips, and he wasn't smiling as he asked, "And the queen?"

"She fought. Or tried to."

He squeezed her tightly.

"And for that, she was banished. The former Queen Verona is ensconced in the coldest, draftiest castle in the middle of a swamp with a dozen Amazons guarding her night and day. She will *never* leave that place."

"And who is leading this troop of Amazons?"

"Not I," she told him, lifting a hand and placing it on his chest, right above his beating heart. "I oversaw Verona's incarceration, stayed in Grand Falls long enough to make sure Ruprecht's throne was secure and his enemies routed, then resigned my commission."

He peered into her eyes, searching for something, some words she hadn't yet offered. It terrified her, baring herself in such a way, but he had done it first, that day she'd left him at the castle. How could she be any less brave than he had been at that moment, when he couldn't be entirely sure she would return, or what would happen if she failed?

"I love you, Rafe," she whispered. Her voice shook, so she repeated the words. "I love you with every bit of my scarred warrior's heart."

His eyes gleamed as he reached for both her hands. "I love you, too," he said. "I love your warrior's heart and your intelligence and your loyalty and your spirit. I want you forever, Olivia."

"Truly?"

"Oh, yes." They kissed again, softly, then he led her to the couch and pulled her down upon it, cradling her in his lap.

"That question you mentioned, the day I left, are you still going to ask it?" she whispered.

"What question?"

Frowning, she prodded, "Wasn't there something you were going to ask me?"

She distinctly recalled something about a bride and a wedding night and a woman who was so not a virgin anymore.

She, the leader of the Amazons, was holding her breath, waiting for a marriage proposal she had never thought she'd want but now couldn't wait to accept.

He cocked his head in confusion. "I don't follow."

"That day I left, you said that when we were free, you were going to ask me a question." Suddenly fearing she'd misunderstood, she bit the corner of her lip. "Oh. Have you already asked it? When you asked me to come with you?"

"As I recall, I didn't ask you to come with me," he said, tossing off the reply as if it didn't matter. "I *told* you to."

Seeing the twinkle in his eyes, knowing he was doing

this strange thing he called teasing, she tightened her arms and scowled. "Stop it."

"You know, even though you're not an Amazon anymore, you're still really hot when you're mad."

"Rafe Cabot!"

He ignored her, waving down at her body. "Speaking of you not being an Amazon anymore, *please* tell me you get to keep the uniform."

"I'm never going to wear it again after this night if you don't stop teasing me!"

Laughing softly, he kissed her forehead, her cheek, her jaw. Then, finally, he slid out from underneath her, dropping to his knees on the floor.

"Olivia, will you stay with me, always? Will you stop being the guard of a king and settle for being the guard of my heart…as my wife?"

She nodded solemnly, knowing this office, this role, was one she would never want to give up all the days of her life. And though she was not a poet, and had never had use for pretty words, she felt the need, just this once, to speak what she truly felt, right down to her soul.

"I will, Rafe. I'll marry you." She lifted a hand to cup his face. "I'll slay dragons for you. I'll refrain from killing saucy wenches who dare to flirt with you when you sing. Someday I'll have your children."

They shared a tender smile. Then Olivia added one more vow.

"And I'll stay by your side until there's nothing left of either of us but the memory of how very much we loved each other."

Epilogue

And so began the reign of King Ruprecht the Merry.

Once considered a fop and a bit of a fool, the young king proved to be as good and respected a monarch as his own much-loved father had been. He had the old king's happy manner, and none of his wicked mother's evil ways.

His sense of justice became as famous as his sense of fashion, and no other ruler in all the lands could throw a better party. Under his rule, Grand Falls became the most modern of all the kingdoms, being the first in all of Elatyria to introduce such things as electric lights and a place called a movie theater.

Those closest to Ruprecht did notice that, every once in a while, he seemed a bit...changed. Some days, he would appear a little taller, his shoulders a bit more broad, his voice more decisive.

The romantics of the court believed it was because his one true love, denied him all his life due to her status as a commoner—and a former Amazonian—had returned for a lengthy visit to her homeland. With her beautiful children in tow, she had to be a sad reminder of the life the bachelor king might have lived.

The more observant members of the court knew better. They saw the depth of warmth and emotion Ruprecht shared with his closest advisor, Jess. And they noted that every time

King Ruprecht seemed to be a different person altogether, Jess would be gone from court for weeks at a time.

None of them knew, of course, that the real Ruprecht, and his dearest love Jess, left once in a year to headline in Vegas. Or that his handsome double covered for the king because of their long-standing friendship.

As for the Amazon warrior and her rock-and-roll singing husband, they lived a long and happy life together in a place called California in the kingdom of the U.S.A. While she went to work catching villains as a city constable, he built her a beautiful chalet overlooking the bay. Together, they filled it with several children.

And every other Saturday, on something they called "date night," she would dig out her old leather skirt and top, and her sexy spike-heeled boots. Then her knight in shining armor would carry her to his tower and remind the warrior princess what being a woman was all about.

For everyone who is still waiting for their own
happily-ever-after.

GOLDIE AND THE THREE BROTHERS
Jennifer LaBrecque

Prologue

THE DIAMOND SOLITAIRE'S facets sparkled in the overhead fluorescent lighting of Ardmore Winery's executive office suite.

"It's beautiful," Goldie Dawkins admired, not even trying to keep the wistful note out of her voice.

Lauren, who wore the winery's administrative assistant hat, rocked her hand back and forth. "It is, isn't it? Now, we've got to find you a guy."

Both in their late twenties, Goldie and Lauren had gotten to know one another fairly well in the two months Goldie had been in and out of the office at the winery while Ardmore decided if she was the right marketing consultant for their expanding enterprise north of metropolitan Atlanta. They had and she was. Yay for her. Now she was just waiting to get in to meet with Ardmore's Chief Operating Officer, Chad Malone.

Ardmore's founder had left the winery to his three nephews, all brothers, when he'd retired two years ago. The oldest nephew, Chad pretty much handled the business end. He'd been her primary contact. Getting an appointment wasn't easy, but she'd always found Chad to be efficient and fairly easy to work with. She'd also met briefly with Scott, the middle brother, who was in charge of shipping and distribution. However, she had yet to meet the youngest brother, Jake, who handled Ardmore's sales. But that would soon change. Jake was slated to sit in on the marketing launch meeting this afternoon.

Goldie leaned against the edge of Lauren's neatly organized desk. "Finding a guy isn't so much the problem," Goldie said.

Lauren knew about Goldie's split with her long-term boyfriend. After a year and a half, Goldie had wanted to take their relationship to the next level. Brett had been happy with the status quo. She wanted a permanent relationship, roots, someone to stand by her through thick and thin. He claimed to love her but only wanted to live together. Unfortunately, before Brett, she'd wasted nearly two years in another dead-end relationship. And since Goldie absolutely refused to repeat her mother's mistake of finding a man who wasn't willing to stick around when a kid showed up, it was sayonara Brett.

"I'm done with commitment-phobic men. Finding a guy who's not absolutely terrified at the concept of marriage seems to be a lost cause."

"Speaking of which—" Lauren looked beyond Goldie "—here's the original lost cause."

Perplexed, Goldie glanced over her shoulder. She found herself gazing into a pair of obsidian eyes with a wicked gleam fringed in equally dark lashes, a straight nose, and the most sensually lush mouth she'd ever seen on a man. A sudden rushing filled her ears, her heart pounded, and she could've sworn the floor tilted beneath her feet.

"Lost cause? You wound me, Lauren." Those dark-as-sin eyes seemed to look straight into Goldie's soul. "Jake Malone," he said by way of introduction, extending a hand.

"Goldie Dawkins." His hand enveloped hers and it took

a moment for her to find her voice again. "It's a pleasure to meet you."

"Likewise." He released her hand and quirked an amused eyebrow at Lauren. "And exactly why am I a lost cause?"

"It's that confirmed-bachelor anti-marriage status of yours."

"There is that." He nodded his head toward Lauren's engagement ring. "I'd say you're the lost cause. I've tried to steer you away from the dark side but you seem intent to self-destruct."

Lauren sent a mock despairing glance Goldie's way. "See? A total lost cause. You can strike him off your potential husband list."

Jake looked at Goldie as if she'd morphed into Medusa. Goldie could've throttled Lauren on the spot. "You have a potential husband list?" he asked in disbelief.

She sounded like a nutcase when he put it that way. Instead she was simply a woman who wanted what she hadn't grown up with: a stable family where a man and woman shared a commitment. "Not actually a list...." Well, there was kind of a list, but that was none of his business.

"She's a modern woman who isn't afraid to say she wants to get married," Lauren said.

"I'm sure you won't have any trouble finding a husband if that's what you want." Well, that was actually very flattering. "After all, there's a sucker born every day."

Jake Malone didn't need to worry about making her list. In less than five minutes he'd gone from being the sexiest man she'd ever laid eyes on to a guy she wouldn't touch with a ten-foot pole. No matter how much she might want to.

1

Six months later...

WHY COULDN'T MEN JUST do what they were supposed to do, be where they were supposed to be, and be there on time? Obviously that was too much to ask, Goldie Dawkins silently fumed as she stood, drenched from the rain, on the front porch of a godforsaken cabin in the middle of the god-forsaken woods in the midst of a godforsaken torrential downpour thunderstorm.

She double-checked the address. Yep. This was the cabin owned by the Malone brothers. She was here, but where were they? As a rivulet of water ran down her cheek, she held on to her temper. It was her enthusiasm and willingness to go the extra mile that had landed her the Ardmore Winery account six months ago. So when Chad, Ardmore's COO, had asked her to "stop by" the cabin to review the latest focus group results with him and Scott, she'd agreed even though it would've been infinitely easier for her to meet at their office.

Sure, she'd just happen to be on the side of a north Georgia mountain late on a Friday afternoon in May and she could drop in. Not. But Chad, a bonafide workaholic if she'd ever met one, had planned a working weekend at the cabin, which according to Lauren, belonged to all three brothers. That was where he wanted to meet, so this was where they were meeting.

Goldie had sat through the traffic from hell getting out of Atlanta, even though she'd left early. Knowing she'd never finish up and get back to her apartment in time to make her Friday night spin class, she'd had the bright idea she'd get her workout by hiking the two miles from the mountain base to the Malone cabin. It hadn't been bad...until two miles as the crow flies turned into more like four on mountainous switchbacks. And then the rain had started. There'd been thunderstorms the past couple of days, but she'd thought they were over. Heck, it had been nice and sunny when she'd started out. Lightning popped nearby, followed by a crash of thunder, and she nearly jumped out of her skin.

She'd endured all of that and now no one was here. And it was still raining to beat the band. All of this for a half-hour meeting, forty-five minutes tops. Where were Chad and Scott?

There was much to admire about Chad: he had a work ethic that wouldn't quit—actually, he was probably the picture Webster used to illustrate the word *workaholic* in their dictionary—and he was certainly good-looking. Great work ethic, if a tad inconsiderate; handsome in a type-A, big-man kind of way—the kind of guy you could depend on. Except, apparently, now.

She peered in through the window of the obviously empty cabin as the rain continued to come down in sheets. It was strange that Scott, brother number two, wasn't here either. Scott Malone was muscled, seriously muscled, and was also quite handsome. Scott was what you'd call the über-athlete. Not only in charge of the distribution depart-ment, he also headed the winery's softball team. Like

Chad, Scott qualified as a good guy. Maybe he was a little too competitive, but he was still a sweetie.

Goldie fished in her purse for her phone. Maybe they'd gotten stuck in traffic. The only bright spot from where she stood was the fact that Jake wasn't supposed to be here. Jake was tied up in an out-of-town sales meeting, which suited her just fine. Jake rattled her cage. He had from the moment she'd met him. And unfortunately for her, every time she'd run into him ever since. Not good, not good at all. She wanted a husband, a family. And from the get-go, it had been apparent that Jake Malone didn't do long-term commitment. So her heart's habit of doing the cha-cha whenever he was around was just plain stupid. She figured sooner or later, like maybe the next millennium, she'd become immune to his dark-as-sin eyes and smile that quirked up the right corner of his mouth. In the meantime, though, she simply stayed the heck away from him.

She hauled out her cell phone. Ack! Still no signal. Blasted cell phone towers. They could send an unmanned vehicle to Mars but they couldn't get a cell phone signal to reach the north Georgia mountains. She paced to the other end of the porch. A beep went off. Ah, music to her ears, it was the sound of her cell phone picking up a signal. She froze and didn't dare move, afraid she'd lose service again. Her message alert promptly went off. She had three voice mails and two text messages.

She pulled up the texts first.

Meeting cancelled. Chad and Scott in 10 car pileup on I-575. Not hurt. Please acknowledge.

She scrolled to the next screen, which essentially repeated the previous message. The three voice mails were from Lauren, who sounded increasingly frantic to reach her.

She pressed Lauren on her contact list. Her friend answered on the second ring.

"Thank God you called. I've been worried sick about you," Lauren said without preamble. Apparently her caller ID had pegged Goldie as the caller. "Are you okay?"

"Other than being soaked to the skin, I'm fine. I got here early so I could hike up the mountain, you know, get in a little exercise, on my way to the meeting. I hadn't counted on losing cell phone service in the mountains…or the rain."

"This is a disaster," Lauren wailed on the other end. "Scott and Chad are stuck on I-575. Traffic is snarled and it's going to be hours before the police sort it out."

What was it with Atlanta drivers when it rained? They lost their minds. The errant thought chased through Goldie's mind as she wrapped her arms around herself. Now that she'd stopped moving, she was freezing in her wet clothes.

Goldie tried to keep her teeth from chattering as she mustered a cheerful tone to soothe Lauren. "It isn't exactly a disaster. They weren't hurt. I'm not hurt. All's well enough. I'll just hike back down to my car and—"

"You haven't heard?"

She didn't know what *it* was, but from Lauren's tone, *it* didn't sound good. "Heard what?"

"Your area is under a tornado watch."

Her control slipped and her teeth did chatter. "Tornado?"

"Well, it's a watch, not a warning. A warning is when…"

Goldie zoned out, struggling to tamp back rising hysteria. Frogs, lizards, toads, snakes, spiders…all those things that terrified many females didn't faze her. Tornados, however, struck a deep and abiding fear into her otherwise intrepid heart. Well, that and psychopaths. Fortunately, she'd yet to encounter a psychopath, or a tornado for that matter, and she'd like to keep it that way.

"…you should be fine if you do that."

Goldie was lost. "Do what?"

"Stay at the cabin until the storm passes and the flash-flood warnings subside."

"Flash-flood warnings?"

"Your phone must've cut out when I was giving you the weather update. There are tornado and flash-flood warnings for the area you're in. Look, there's not a prayer Scott and Chad are going to make it up there tonight. And Maisie Watts, the local woman who comes in and cleans and stocks the cabin before the guys use it, was there this morning. There are clean sheets and food inside. You might as well make use of it. Do you see the bag of checkers sitting on the checker table on the porch?" Sure enough, to Goldie's left, between two rocking chairs, was a table with a checker top and a worn leather draw bag sitting on the table's corner.

"I see it."

"Dump out the checkers and there's a key to the front door in the bottom of the bag. Let yourself in and just stay there tonight. Heck, you could even stay for the weekend, if you wanted. Chad's going to waste half of his day tomorrow picking up a rental car and dealing with his insurance company."

"You're sure they wouldn't mind?"

"I'm sure. Besides, since they won't get up there this weekend, the food will just go to waste. There's no sense in that."

Goldie was cold—freezing, come to think of it—wet and kind of terrified at the notion of getting sucked up in a funnel cloud or drowning in a flash flood. Making herself at home in someone else's place had never appealed to her, but it sounded pretty darn good about now.

"Hold on," Goldie said, putting the phone on the rail.

She spilled the checkers onto the table and fished out the key in the waning light. Her fingers were so cold, it was difficult to hold on to the metal. She picked the phone back up. "Got it. I'm going in."

JAKE MALONE HELD HIS cell phone against one ear as he paid for a cup of coffee at New York's bustling LaGuardia airport. He filled Chad in. "That's right. Even though my meeting with Wayne Tatum got bumped because of food poisoning, his secretary placed the order for me." He side-stepped a woman pushing a stroller and dragging a screaming toddler along. Hopefully he wouldn't be sitting next to them on his flight back to Atlanta. "He was impressed with what I had to say over dinner last night. I talked briefly about our quality control and our pricing structure. His secretary said I was gracious about the meeting being cancelled, and that held a lot of sway with Wayne."

"Good deal," Chad said. "That'll have a nice effect on our fourth quarter P&L."

Jake was pleased. It had taken some time for him, as the perpetually little brother, to find his place, his way in the family pecking order and the family business. But he was damn good at what he did—sales. That wasn't arrogance, that was simply surety in his own sense of self. He'd finally realized he was good at figuring out what made people tick and that went a long way in bolstering his career. Work and the bottom line made Chad tick.

"Yep, I thought it was a nice wrap to what looked like a lost trip." He'd figured the flight up to New York had been a write-off when Tatum had gotten sick. And then to add insult to injury, Jake's last-minute flight out of LaGuardia had been cancelled, which meant he had a couple of hours to kill in the airport.

"At least one of us got something accomplished today," Chad said. "Scott and I got caught in a pileup on I-575 on our way to the cabin."

Jake swore. "How's the car?" Obviously both Scott and Chad were fine or Chad would've mentioned otherwise.

"It needs some work. Hopefully the insurance company won't write it off. But it meant cancelling our meeting with Goldie Dawkins."

Simply hearing her name, Jake tensed. He usually knew when she was going to be in the office and he made sure he wasn't around. It was best not to put himself in the path of a woman who made no bones about wanting a ring on her finger. Funny, she was one of the few people he didn't have a handle on, which might explain why it took a fair amount of willpower on his part to avoid her. But avoid her he did—like the plague. "I didn't know you two were meeting with her."

"Yeah, we were supposed to go over focus group results late this afternoon. It was going to be a working weekend."

"She was spending the whole weekend with you there?" The thought of Chad and Goldie spending that much time at the cabin slammed into him like a fist in the gut. Jake might not want to date a marriage-minded woman, but he damn sure didn't like the idea of Chad being with her.

"No. She was just dropping by for the meeting." A sharp note of warning entered Chad's voice. "I never mix business and pleasure."

Which would explain why Chad seldom dated. Jake's big brother was all about business—including minding his two younger brothers' business, apparently. But Chad could save the slightly admonishing warning as far as Jake was concerned. Goldie Dawkins could show up naked in front of him—which he was pretty damn sure would be stimulating—and he'd still turn around and walk away. The very thought of matrimony made him shudder.

When had he actually taken a vow of bachelorhood? Damned if he could remember the exact time. It was something that had just sort of developed over the years as he witnessed the fights and arguments between two people who should never have married but stayed together "for the kids"—his parents. God knows "the kids" were old enough now, so he could only surmise that his parents stayed miserable together out of habit. At this juncture, it didn't matter. Jake knew without any measure of doubt that he never wanted to enter the esteemed battleground commonly known as marriage. He liked women, respected them. He wasn't a player. He was a great boyfriend, but he was straight-up about his intentions with any woman he ever dated. And since it was a husband Goldie Dawkins wanted, he didn't give a damn how attracted to her he was—and he was, to the point that once or twice he'd been tempted to forget his rule and ask her out, but sanity and good sense had always prevailed—he'd stayed away.

Regardless, Jake felt something perilously close to relief that Chad and Goldie hadn't planned a cozy weekend at the cabin. "Are you going to try to get up there tomorrow?"

"No. I ditched the idea altogether, especially since there are flash-flood warnings. It doesn't make sense to take a rental through there." The cabin's remoteness had been part of the appeal when Jake, Chad and Scott had decided to go in together and buy the place. The north Georgia mountains had become increasingly popular for cabin rentals and weekend getaways. Some areas were damn near as crowded as Altanta's suburbs, but Hawk's Nest was one of the few places where you could truly escape. "You're not thinking about heading up, are you?"

"I wasn't, but maybe I should," Jake said. "Did Maisie stock the place?" Since he'd planned to be in New York until Saturday morning, he hadn't made any other plans.

"She stocked it and cleaned, but the creeks might be tricky."

The more Jake thought about it, the better a relaxing weekend up in mountains sounded. "Hey, tricky means fun. That's why I have a four-wheel drive." His Toyota FJ Cruiser was mostly wasted in the city. Crossing a swollen Rotter's Creek, however, was what it was made for.

"Go for it, then," Chad said, distraction evident in his voice. No doubt he was reading through some report or another.

"See you," Jake said, ending the call.

He checked the clock on his phone. Perfect. By the time his flight got into the city, rush hour would be over. With a bit of luck, he should be there early in the evening.

A little R&R alone at Hawk's Nest was just what he needed.

2

ONE PUSH AND THE DARK green door opened on well-oiled hinges. Goldie was about to step inside when she realized she was puddling water all over the front mat.

Lauren might tell her the Malones wouldn't care if she stayed there, but she'd rather not trek water through the place. She made quick work of wringing out her hair and stripping out of her sopping wet clothes. Gooseflesh prickled her skin as she left the clothes heaped on the porch and stepped naked into the cabin. She closed the door behind her, shutting out the driving rain that noisily pinged against the dwelling's tin roof.

A quick glance revealed the cabin's layout. Kitchen to the left, with an opening facing the great room and fireplace. To the right, a short hallway led to what were probably the bedrooms.

The wooden floors were scattered with rugs and the walls and ceiling were paneled with knotty pine. In the corner, a large stone fireplace with a flat-screen TV mounted above it beckoned while three recliners tempted her to make herself at home.

Goldie headed straight to the hallway, her breasts bouncing along without the support of her bra, her nipples tight and hard from the chill of the rain.

The bathroom door stood open. The room was nothing

fancy, but the white tile floor was clean, as was the sink and toilet.

She opened the narrow door that had to be a linen closet. She pulled out a thick, white, oversize bath sheet and wrapped it around her sarong-wise. Taking another towel, she wrapped it around her shoulders like a shawl. Finally the gooseflesh prickling her skin began to dissipate. She stepped over to the tub and began filling it with warm water.

Outside, a crash of thunder shook the whole cabin and she was pretty sure the clatter against the tin roof was hail. Hail wasn't a good sign. Hail meant tornadoes.

She hurried back to the den and grabbed the TV remote. Okay, Weather Channel…Weather Channel… Come on, where was the flipping Weather Channel…ah, there it was. An update ran across the bottom of the screen, listing all the counties under a tornado watch. Hallelujah. Her area was only slated for thunderstorms.

She relaxed a bit, but the truth of the matter was her nerves were shot. Between the hike, the cancelled meeting, getting drenched and the tornado threat, she was ready to jump out of her skin. Lauren had told her to make herself at home—well, if she hadn't used those exact words, the implication had been there. Although she wasn't much of a drinker, Goldie sure needed a drink now. She ducked back into the bathroom to check the tub. It was almost full. She turned off the water and made her way to the kitchen.

Opening the refrigerator, she smiled. The Malone brothers might run a winery, but they obviously preferred beer. And not even the fancy stuff at that.

Without blinking twice, she snagged one. She'd replace it. She turned and hesitated. What the heck? She grabbed another can.

A brew in each hand, she retraced her steps to the

bathroom. Placing the brews on the side of the tub, she shed the towels, stepped in and sank into the enveloping warmth of the water. Ah…heavenly bliss. Even though it was May, the rain had been cold and she was chilled to the bone. Closing her eyes, she slid down until immersed completely, except for her knees, letting her hair float around her head like seaweed.

How many times had she done this very thing as a child, pretending she was a mermaid? More than she could count. And color her a romantic, she still believed in magic and fairy-tale endings.

She lifted her head from the water and settled against the back of the tub, wiping water from her eyes. Goldie popped the top and took a long pull from the can. The cold beer offered a nice contrast to the warm bath. If the weather shifted and a tornado came along and transported her to some farmer's field in the valley, she might as well have a little buzz going and be clean when she died.

Eager to forget about the storm outside, she distracted herself with thoughts of the Malone brothers. Actually, there was something rather decadent about sitting naked in their tub without their knowledge.

She took another swig of her beer and propped her feet on the other end of the tub. Given a choice, which brother did she wish was in the bath with her now? Definitely not all three. Her college friend, Lissa, had been into the whole ménage scene, but it had never appealed to Goldie. Goldie wanted her men one at a time. So…hmm…which one?

Chad? A woman could rely on Chad. She closed her eyes and imagined him behind her, his chest pillowing her back, his thighs cradling her buttocks. Unfortunately, the immediate thought that chased that scenario was him instructing her on how to sit so they could accomplish their bath as efficiently as possible. She winced. She found it highly probable the workaholic Chadster would approach making love as a task to be accomplished before moving on to the next item on his To-Do list.

She shook her head and took another long swallow. She'd better drink fast because she only liked beer cold.

Brother number two, then. Nice, safe Scott with his sandy blond hair and green eyes. He was a little on the short side but he was so powerfully built, it more than compensated. She envisioned Scott sitting opposite her. Unbidden, in her mind's eye, she saw him reach over the side of the tub and grab a stopwatch while he announced he was timing them to see if he could beat his last time. *That* made her laugh. Once again, as with Chad, she probably wasn't too far off the mark.

Which left the notion of dangerously handsome Jake climbing in with her. It was an equal mix of desperation and reckless abandon that led her to pop the second can and polish off almost half of it in one swallow. Jake had spelled trouble for her from the moment she'd met him.

Jake. He was tall, but not as tall and beefy as Chad, and not as vertically challenged as Scott. She estimated Jake to be around six feet with nice broad shoulders that narrowed to a trim waist and yes, his ass appeared to be tight. What the heck? She was female and breathing, so she'd noticed once, or twice, or maybe every darn time she happened to walk behind him in the hallway. Dark brown hair and olive-tinted skin. But it was his eyes that did her in. Those eyes of his were so inky black it was impossible to tell the demarcation between pupil and iris.

But even outside the very nice physical attributes—and make no doubt about it, they were nice—Jake aroused something inside her that made her want to abandon her resolve, her goals and take a walk on the wild side. And that was just plain stupid considering she'd grown up with a mother who'd done just that. So, she steadfastly avoided Jake in the flesh…but after two beers and a warm bubble bath in his remote cabin, she decided there was no need to avoid Jake in her imagination. What the heck? Why not take a mental walk on the wild side with the man she wanted most but couldn't have?

She lathered up the washcloth and rubbed it over her shoulders and the top of her back, the soap's scent faintly reminiscent of Jake. It was as if his smell was imprinted on her skin, marking her as his, which was totally fanciful. They'd never even exchanged more than a few words. Nonetheless, that's what it was like.

Eyes closed, she slid down until the warm water lapped the same path she'd soaped. She could almost feel the sensation of his hair-roughened chest against her back, the press of his fingertips against her shoulders, the whisper of his warm breath against her neck. She sighed, sliding deeper into the water and her fantasy.

The delicious scrape of his beard against her sensitive neck heralded his kiss. Almost nothing felt better than the play of his lips along her neck, across her shoulder. He cupped her jaw in his hand and turned her head until his mouth claimed hers, his other hand sliding beneath the water to cup her breasts, his fingers finding her aching tips.

Arousal overwhelmed her as his hand slid farther down her nakedness, over the slight curve of her belly and the rounded line of her hip, only to trace back along her inner thigh to the spot that quivered in anticipation of his touch.

He explored her, stroked her, teased her until their mingled breath came in short gasps and she found her release.

She floated in the water for a moment and then blinked

her eyes open. The harsh bathroom light jarred her back into reality. She was alone in the tub, which was simultaneously a pity and a relief. It wasn't the first time she'd imagined making love with Jake Malone. The pity of it was that she was almost certain he'd be better in the flesh than in her imagination. And that was already pretty darn good. The relief was it was much wiser and much safer to indulge in fantasy than in flesh when it came to the commitment-phobic Jake.

That thought left her feeling slightly disconcerted, rather than satisfied. Goldie finished her bath and dried off in record time.

She could walk around naked or she could borrow a shirt until she could wash and dry her clothes that were currently piled on the front porch. Hanging the towel on the rack, she made an executive decision to borrow. Still, she was determined not to be a needy nutcase and make a bee-line for Jake's clothes.

She opened the first door to the right outside of the bathroom and knew without a doubt it was Chad's bedroom. Everything was scrupulously tidy. She padded across to the closet, where she found everything organized by color. It also immediately struck her that the guy didn't even own a T-shirt. Collared golf shirts hung next to a couple of button-downs—who wore button-downs at a cabin in the woods? Obviously Chad Malone did. But there wasn't a single T-shirt to be found. Okay. Never mind.

She closed the closet and moved on to the next bedroom. It wasn't exactly a disaster area but the room certainly qualified as being messy. Sneakers and water shoes sat piled in one corner. Scott would definitely have T-shirts. That was all she wanted—a warm, dry shirt to cover her. She opened his closet and wrinkled her nose at the faint odor of sweat. Er...no.

Okay, throw in another qualifier. A warm, dry, non-stinky T-shirt. Come to think of it, Scott did sort of always smell as if he needed a shower. She'd pass on his shirts.

Which left her one choice. Needy nutcase or not, she was going to have to turn to Jake—well, at least his room for now.

She opened the third bedroom and every nerve ending in her body sensed his energy. It was as if her inner radar was tuned into his particular frequency, which was just flat-out annoying. Nonetheless, she opened his closet and yanked out the first T-shirt she saw, a worn cotton advertising a 2006 blues festival. It hit her midthigh. And dammit all to hell, his T-shirt smelled like him. Maybe she'd be better off walking around naked. But sitting bare-bottomed on the furniture just seemed…well, tacky.

Feeling unusually defiant, possibly—make that probably—due to drinking two brews on a nearly empty stomach followed by feeling the slide of Jake's cotton T-shirt against her bare skin, she marched back to the den. Her wet clothes were piled on the front porch but what did it matter? She was warm and dry now. Why fool around with wet, cold clothes? After all, she'd already let herself into their cabin, drank their beer, used their bath and helped herself to Jake's T-shirt—why not traipse back to the den and check out more than the Weather Channel on the television while she was at it?

If a little karma happened to be coming her way, they'd have satellite and she could catch reruns of *The Tudors*. Heaven help her and the rest of the women in TV Land, but Henry Cavill was hot, hot, hot.

She stopped midway down the short hallway. Jake. That was who he looked like—Henry Cavill as the Duke of Suffolk. Why hadn't she made the connection before? A shiver ran down her spine. Was that why she liked watching

The Tudors so much? Was that why that scene between Henry Cavill and Gabrielle Anwar turned her on? Could she watch it over and over and over again because it was Jake she was plugging in there?

Absolutely not. She was just being weird because she was in the man's space wearing his T-shirt and she'd recently pleasured herself in his bathtub. But she was not addicted to *The Tudors* because of him. Definitely not. That would mean she had some kind of thing for him and she most definitely did not. Nope. She had too much sense to have a thing for Jake Malone.

Feeling a little strange at rummaging through the Malones' cabin, Goldie nonetheless heeded her stomach's rumbling and checked out the fridge contents. Deli ham, turkey and roast beef. Sliced swiss and cheddar cheese. Deli potato salad. Eggs. Precooked bacon. A container of fresh fruit. Wings.

Goldie paused. She loved wings but she almost never ate them. They were too fattening. She should prepare an omelette and haul out the fruit for a nice healthy dinner. She reached for the fruit container and then hesitated. The wings looked so good and this was like a little mini-vacation, wasn't it? Okay, mini-vacation was a stretch, but she was stuck here for the night, so maybe she could bend her normal rules a bit.

Temptation tapped her on her shoulder. She always did the right thing, made good choices. And after all, she had burned a few calories hiking up here. The wings and beer called her name. Spying blue cheese dressing next to carrots and celery sticks, she was a goner. She gave up the ghost of a healthy, low-fat dinner and hauled out the wings, dressing and carrots. Life was good. She hoped the wings weren't plain, or worse, hot enough to burn your mouth off.

She dipped her finger into a smidgen of sauce on the container bottom. Yum. Just right.

Humming Michael Bublé's "Call Me Irresponsible" beneath her breath, she found aluminum foil and turned the oven on. Then she wrapped the wings up, popped them inside and set the timer. Reheating wings in a microwave was just wrong.

While she was waiting, she decided to check out the rest of the cabin. She felt more than a little invasive, but she was here and her curiosity outweighed her conscience. Heck, it wasn't as if she was riffling through drawers or reading personal correspondence. She was just checking out the general decor.

Framed photos hung on one of the timbered walls. There was one of the Malone brothers all hoisting white-water paddles with a raft "parked" on a riverbank behind them. Her gaze lingered on Jake. He wore an exuberant boyish grin, his enthusiasm a near palpable force.

A familiar tingle coursed through her and she wondered, for about the fifty-millionth time, what had soured him on marriage. And for the fifty-millionth time she reminded herself that the reason didn't matter. What mattered was that he was as set against commitment as she was determined to have it.

In another frame, an older couple who had to be the Malones' parents stood against the backdrop of the Grand Canyon's south rim. Hmm. Jake had his mother's facial shape but his coloring was his father's. She leaned her head to one side, studying the photo. Something wasn't quite right. Then it hit her. Both of his parents—make that *their,* Chad, Scott and Jake—were smiling, but Mrs. Malone's eyes were sad and Mr. Malone's eyes portrayed anger. Despite the smiles, Goldie would guess they weren't a happy couple.

Another photo featured a wet dog—some type of lab/retriever mix—sitting on the edge of a lake wearing a lopsided canine smile. Goldie felt herself returning the dog's infectious grin. She'd been thinking about getting a dog. When she'd worked for Young, Blarnsworth and Felders Marketing, Inc., she'd traveled too much to have a dog. Then when she'd started her own consulting business she'd been gone too much, as well. But now, Goldie's client base was right on target with where she wanted to be and didn't necessitate nearly as much travel. And recently, she'd been thinking of checking out the local animal rescue to find her own furry friend.

She glanced back to the photo of Jake, Chad and Scott. Technically Scott was better looking, but Jake owned the sexy element hands down. A tight knot of desire clenched low in her belly. He had the most beautifully sensual mouth she'd ever seen on a man—firm, sculpted lips that looked as if they could kiss a woman and her various parts insensible. Best not to go there.

She turned her attention back to the remaining photos—three "nature shots." One of the fall leaves in shades of golds, reds and oranges; one of a hawk circling and the third a mountain stream with heavy-laden boughs of mountain laurel dipping almost to the stream's edge. It wasn't even a conscious thought—instead there was a "knowing" inside her. These were Jake's photographs. Chad was too focused on all things work-related to be into nature photography and Scott would be too busy hiking or mountain biking or kayaking a whitewater river. These had to be Jake's.

She turned away abruptly, almost sorry she'd seen them. She didn't want to know this about him. It was like taking an intimate peek into his soul. And Jake's soul was none of her business.

She crossed the room and checked out the chairs arranged in a semicircle in front of the fireplace and television. It was sort of cool there was no sofa in the room—just three recliners. She plopped into one. Nope. Too big, and the fabric was sort of itchy against the backs of her legs. The darn thing practically swallowed her. She moved on to the second one. Uh-uh. It had some funky lumbar-support thingy that hit her awkwardly and the leather was cracked along one side. She sank into the third chair—big, but not too big. And the microfiber material felt soft and cozy. Nice. Just right.

The timer went off and she retraced her steps to the kitchen. Five minutes later, she was settled in the comfy recliner, eating wings, drinking another beer and watching *The Office.* No Tudors for her tonight. She finished up her dinner and realized that between the hike, the food and drink and the warm bath, she was ready to call it a night.

Exactly how it happened, she wasn't sure, but she grabbed the handle on the side of the recliner to lower the footrest and the thing came off in her hand. Horrified, she stared at it for a second. She was no mechanical genius but surely she could fix it.

She scooted forward and stood up. Well, maybe there was a little bit of a stagger, because truth be told, that third beer had gone straight to her head. She knelt on the braided rug and tried to repair the chair, but she simply couldn't see a way to reattach the handle. Leaving the piece on the floor next to the recliner, she stood. She'd try again tomorrow morning. She'd be more clearheaded after a good night's sleep.

But the least she could do was put the footrest down. Goldie tried to toe it back into place, only she used a little too much force. One second the chair was fine, well, as fine as it could be without a handle, and the next, it wasn't.

Staring as it listed drunkenly to one side, she giggled. Double oops. She'd just trashed the only comfy chair in the house. Granted, she hadn't meant to, but it was trashed nonetheless.

What the heck? It was only eight-thirty but she thought she'd better go to bed before she screwed anything else up. After all, she couldn't get into trouble in bed.

"FINALLY," JAKE MALONE muttered aloud as he pulled into the unpaved driveway, the headlights picking out the cabin's welcoming front porch.

His flight had gotten in from New York so late he'd almost changed his mind about coming up. And then there'd been the woman…

He hadn't particularly wanted to change the minivan's flat tire on the side of the road in the pouring rain, but there'd been no way in hell he could feel good about driving past the lady when his headlights picked her out on the side of the road in the dark. The woman didn't look as if she knew one end of a jack from another, and her three little kids had been hanging out of the window watching her when he passed.

He'd pulled over and changed the tire for her. She'd been a single mom, newly divorced, and so damn grateful he'd practically had to get back in his truck and drive away to escape being thanked to death. He was cold, wet and hungry. And while four-wheeling through swollen Rotter's Creek had been fun, he was relieved he hadn't gotten stuck. He patted the dash of his trusty FJ Cruiser. Four-wheel drive on the fly was a beautiful thing, but another half hour and not even the Cruiser could've handled Rotter's Creek. He was definitely here for the weekend. There'd be no crossing that creek again until the water levels receded. He was more than ready for a hot shower, a cold brew, some TV time and his own bed.

He parked close to the porch and hauled his overnight case and briefcase out of the backseat. He took the two front steps in one stride. Unlocking the front door, he damn near tripped going in. What the hell? He reached inside next to the door and flipped on the front porch light. A pile of wet clothes, most notably a pair of red-and-black panties and a matching bra, sat heaped in front of the door.

Word had circulated in their mountain community about a rash of break-ins in the last couple of months. Most of the cabins up here were weekend retreats, and while things hadn't been stolen, there'd been vandalism. Everyone was pretty sure teenagers were behind it, but nonetheless it was breaking and entering. If some teenage boy had brought his girlfriend up here for a good time, they'd both be in for it. The idea of someone invading his retreat pissed him off to no end.

Quietly, carefully, he placed his bags on the floor and looked around. Son of a bitch. He was about to have a reckoning with someone. *His* recliner sat broken in the den.

Jake stepped out of his wet shoes. He could move more quietly through the house in his socks. And while everyone suspected teenagers were behind the mischief—and there was obviously a female involved—he still needed a weapon. Bottom line, he didn't know who or what he was going to find.

Jake grabbed the fire iron by the hearth and checked the kitchen, his nose picking up the smell of hot wings.

Opening the cabinet under the sink, he caught sight of chicken wing bones and empty beer cans in the garbage. He tightened his hand around the iron poker, his temper rising. His chair was broken, his wings and beer gone…and if the culprits weren't in here, that only left the bedrooms.

The bathroom door stood ajar, the light on, the way his mom had done for him and his brothers when they'd stayed in a hotel or their grandparents' beach cottage. He shook his head. Just his luck to find vandals too chickenshit to sleep without a nightlight in the bathroom. Well, they were about to get a rude awakening.

He eased open Chad's bedroom door. Empty. Scott's room was next. Empty, as well. Which left his room.

Heart thumping, adrenaline pumping, he slipped into the room. Bingo.

In the darkness, he made out a lump in his bed. The element of surprise would be to his advantage. He flipped on the overhead light. "Who the hell are you and why the hell are you in my bed?" he yelled.

A woman jacked up in the bed, screaming bloody murder.

In rapid succession Jake discerned two critical pieces of information.

One: blond-haired, blue-eyed Goldie Dawkins was alone in his bed.

And two: she was gloriously naked.

3

"YOU SCARED THE LIFE out of me," Goldie said, snatching the covers up over her bare breasts and willing her heartbeat to slow down.

"Honey, you're in my bed. You broke my chair. You ate my wings and you drank my beer—" from the scowl drawing his dark brows together over his dark eyes, she figured that was the worst of her infractions "—but let me apologize for giving you a fright while you're cozied up in my bed."

She'd tried all three beds. Chad's bed was too hard. She had no idea how Scott's back ever survived the lack of support in his mattress. Unfortunately, Jake's bed had felt just right. But put that way… "I can explain."

He propped the iron next to the door and leaned against the frame, crossing his arms over his chest. "I'm sure you can. I can't wait to hear this."

Despite what had been actually said, there was a current of powerful attraction running between them. They both knew she was naked in his bed. In fact, pertinent parts of her were tingling and tightening in response now that the initial terror of having a crazy person with a weapon invading the bedroom was over. Tingling and tightening was bad business. If he had any idea of that fantasy she'd had about him in the tub earlier this evening… She swallowed hard.

"Why don't you put on some clothes," he said, his voice low and strained, his dark eyes unfathomable.

"I was just about to say that very thing." Well, she would've when her brain had returned to normal function, she was sure of it. "Putting on some clothes is an excellent plan. Only, all I've got is that T-shirt that's on the floor, and um…it's yours. My clothes are—" She sounded like an idiot and it was all his fault.

He interrupted her stumbling spiel. "Piled wet at the front door. I know. I damn near broke my neck coming in."

He didn't look happy. Well, big whoop. She wasn't happy either. Not by a long shot. Jake Malone was the last person on the planet she'd want to be alone and naked with in this cabin. Well, except for maybe a deranged psychopath.

"Excuse me for being thoughtful. I didn't want to drip water all over the floor. And I was assured no one would be here this weekend. You're supposed to be in New York." As a consultant, she technically worked for his company, but that didn't mean she had to take any crap from him. Sheet clutched over her bare breasts, she glared back.

"Sorry to interfere with your plans." Humph. The dry sarcasm was totally uncalled for, in her opinion. "Now, would you please put on some clothes, even if they are mine."

She'd never regretted anything as much as she regretted picking one of his shirts. She should've worn one of Scott's stinky ones. However, she hadn't, so… "I would be delighted to put on some clothes…as soon as you turn around. You've just enjoyed your one and only free show for the evening." His surprise turned to a smirk. That had come out all wrong. God, she'd like to slap that smirk right off his sensual, well-shaped, beautiful, male mouth that would feel just right against her… "That came out wrong.

You couldn't pay me enough either." That just made the situation and his amusement even worse. "Oh, shut up—"

"But I haven't said anything."

Thoroughly flustered, she felt a blush burning up her neck and face. "I'm not used to men walking in when I'm naked."

"So I gather. Let me know if you want to practice this again some time." The look in his eyes set her pulse pounding and that disconcerting tightening and tingling intensified as her ever-fertile imagination saw him moving across the room, shedding his clothes, and climbing into bed naked, *with* her. No, no and no. Of all the men in the world, how could she be so stupid as to want *him?*

Exasperated, she snapped, "Just pretend you're a gentleman and turn around so I can get dressed. Better yet, step out of the room and close the door behind you."

"I'll be waiting outside," he said as he turned and left.

Goldie's hands, and her legs for that matter, weren't particularly steady when she climbed out of Jake Malone's bed and pulled on his T-shirt. She looked down the front of the shirt in dismay. There was no mistaking the pebbling of her nipples against the soft, worn cotton. She'd like to blame it on the cold factor but sadly enough, it was the Jake factor. She rubbed her palms over her breasts thinking she could at least mitigate the evidence of her arousal. Nope. Still no better.

The closed door muffled his voice, but she still jumped when he asked, "How long does it take to pull on a T-shirt?"

She wasn't a happy camper. Had he put a move on her, she wouldn't have been pleased—honestly, she *wouldn't* have. But she'd wanted him for months. And so, it bothered her that he'd walked in to find her naked in his bed and instead of stripping down and joining her, he'd merely suggested she get dressed. That didn't do much for a woman's ego, now did it?

She wasn't sure who she was more put out with—him for not wanting her, or her for being put out with him for not wanting her the way she wanted him. And wasn't that a confusing mess? She marched across the room and threw open the door. "Dressed."

His eyes dropped to her chest and the heat he awakened inside her flared into a freaking bonfire as his gaze lingered. It was as if he touched her through the thin fabric and her nipples pearled into even harder tips. Her mouth went dry and her heartbeat set off like a trip hammer at the expression on his face.

He didn't say a word, but stepped around her without touching her. He crossed the room in two strides and pulled open the closet door. In less than a minute, he was back, thrusting a pair of cotton pajama pants with a drawstring waist and a sweatshirt at her. "Put these on in the bathroom while I change into dry clothes in here."

Who did he think he was, ordering her around? "I don't have to—"

He interrupted her again, narrowing his eyes. "I'm trying very hard to be a gentleman. Trust me when I say you and I don't need to be in the same room when you're only wearing a T-shirt. So go into the bathroom and put these on. Now."

A shiver chased down her spine at his commanding tone. Okay, so maybe he wasn't totally immune to her either. She took the clothes from him and ducked into the bathroom, even as she heard his bedroom door click closed behind her. A crazy smile curved her lips. And indeed it was crazy, madness in its finest moment.

Jake had sent her in here to cover herself from head to toe because he was as attracted to her as she was to him. She knew it without a doubt. He wanted her. It had been in his dark eyes and his peremptory tone.

She stepped into his pajama bottoms. They were nothing more than thin striped cotton, but they were his and she felt a frisson of arousal at the brush of his clothes against her. She cinched the drawstring into place and bent down to roll the pants up several times until she could walk without tripping. Then she pulled on his University of Georgia hoodie.

She glanced at herself in the mirror, finger-combing her short blond hair into place. His sleep pants swallowed her and his hoodie fell halfway to her knees. She bit her lower lip but it still didn't stop her smile.

She was covered from head to toe but now, more than ever, she looked as if she'd just crawled out of his bed. And she had. The only problem was that he'd never been in there with her. And that was good. Wasn't it? Absolutely. She even nodded at her own reflection. *But he wanted to be in bed with you,* the insidious voice of temptation whispered into her ear, *otherwise he wouldn't have given you so many clothes to put on.*

And therein lay the road to true madness. But she knew that madness would taste sweet indeed.

JAKE STRIPPED OFF HIS clothes but couldn't seem to look away from the rumpled bed. It had taken every ounce of willpower he possessed not to join her there. He'd wanted to climb up on that mattress, slip beneath the covers and see if her curves would fit as perfectly against his body as he suspected they would.

He pulled on dry underwear and a clean pair of jeans. It wasn't every day that a guy walked in and found a woman he desperately wanted but couldn't have naked in his bed. At least it was a first for him.

Certainly he'd been attracted to women who wanted more than he was willing to offer. It had never been a problem. They'd gone their separate ways and both moved on. But Goldie Dawkins had been an unscratched itch from the moment he met her. He couldn't seem to get her out of his head, but the last place he expected to find her was in his bed. Damn it, she'd been so sexy, so cute with her tousled hair and outrage, clutching his sheet, her shoulders gleaming alabaster in the overhead light's glare.

Jake tried to zip his jeans and discovered that wasn't going to happen right now. He traded them for a loose pair of sweats that did nothing to hide his reaction to the evening's events. Right. He picked out the loosest, longest T-shirt in his closet and pulled it over his head. That was better. And having her covered should help. At least he hoped it would help, because neither one of them was going anywhere tonight.

He scooped up his wet clothes and opened the bedroom door. Goldie exited the bathroom at the same time and they were face-to-face in the tight, close quarters of the dark hall. It was like being thrown into the middle of a storm. Every sense went on heightened alert. Her gaze tangled with his, her eyes widening. She moistened her upper lip with the tip of her pink tongue, and Jake wasn't sure if he could even remember his own name.

Her scent, not her perfume, but her uniqueness, teased him. He longed to trace the soft, feminine curve of her cheek, to memorize the fullness of her lips with his fingers before following the same path with his lips. She looked away first.

"So…um…" She glanced down at her clothes. "Better?"

"Much." He didn't make it a habit to lie, but now seemed to be an occasion that demanded it. No, it wasn't better. He wanted to toss aside his wet clothes, step forward until she was pressed against him intimately, bury his hands in her hair, and lose himself and his conscience in the taste and texture of her mouth.

Instead he deliberately stepped around her, opened the bifold doors that hid the stacking washer/dryer and tossed his clothes into the washer. "Why don't you grab your clothes off the front porch and we'll throw them in, as well," he said. The sooner she was fully clothed in panties and bra and everything else, the better.

She nodded but instead of moving, she stood there, dammit, in front of him. "If you want, I can strip the sheets off your bed and we can wash those, too? Or I can just change them if you have extra linens."

The cabin was a weekend retreat—they kept minimal stuff here. One pair of sheets per bed. "There's no extra linens, but don't worry about it. I'll sleep in one of the other bedrooms or take one of the recliners in the den."

She set her chin at a stubborn angle. "Absolutely not. It's your room and if anyone is going to sleep elsewhere, it'll be me. I can sleep in Chad's room or Scott's."

It was one thing to think of her in his bed and another altogether to think of her in either one of his brothers' beds. The very idea made his gut clench. Over his dead body would she sleep in Scott or Chad's bed, even if they weren't here. "No."

"But, I—"

He didn't know what she was going to say nor did he give a damn. She'd picked his bed and while he might not join her there, like the donning of a horsehair shirt, he wanted her there with a desperation that didn't bear scrutinizing too closely.

He cut off her argument by closing the gap between them and cupping her chin in his palm. Her skin soft and warm beneath his, he tilted her face up. Her mouth, with the soft bow of her upper lip and the fullness of the bottom, issued a siren's call. Just one kiss…one taste of her lips, one measure of her tongue against his. Her lips parted in invitation. He dipped his head. One kiss to satisfy them both. But one kiss would never be enough.

He raised his head and released her at the same time she pulled away.

"Goldie—"

"Jake—"

They spoke at the same time, each halting and then trying again.

"I should—"

"You should—"

Again, they spoke at the same time. They laughed, breaking the sexual tension that had gripped them both. "Ladies first," Jake said.

She stepped around him and tucked her hair behind her ear. "I was just going to say I needed to get my clothes."

He realized with a start that it was raining harder than ever now, the drops dancing against the tin roof with resounding pings. "Right."

She walked to the front door and he followed her. She might need a hand. When she opened the door, he suddenly noticed the temperature had really dropped. The weather could be cold up in the mountains, even in May. In the dark yawning beyond the light spilling outside the door, an owl hooted in the distance.

"Jake, did you move my clothes?"

"No." He stepped into the space behind her and her body heat drew him closer still. In a combination of cold weather and hot woman, his body tightened, his blood quickened.

"They were…right there."

The wood was still dark from the wet pile, which was markedly missing. "Fester," he yelled out into the dark night. "Damn raccoon," he muttered, circling her arm with his fingers and pulling her back inside. He closed the door, blocking out the night and the chill. "You might as well forget it. You won't be getting your clothes tonight."

Amusement sparkled in her blue eyes. "Let me get this straight. You have a clothes-stealing raccoon named Fester?" She laughed, low and husky, tilting her head in disbelief.

She was dead sexy and seriously challenged his resolve. "I don't have him. He's just here." Moving away from her while he still could, Jake crossed to the fireplace and dropped to his haunches. "He's been around for a couple of years." He began to lay a fire. "Typically raccoons only steal shiny stuff or food, but Fester's a freak and he'll make off with anything that's not tied down. He's a pack rat in a raccoon's body."

Goldie propped herself against the cabin's log wall, watching. Jake struck a match and the kindling caught fire. That was precisely how he felt in her presence—like kindling coming into contact with a bright flame.

"Is he named after Uncle Fester on *The Addams Family?*" she said.

He glanced over his shoulder, in surprise and admiration. "Not a lot of people get that."

"I was a total *Addams Family* junkie when I was in high school." Her laugh held a note of self-consciousness. "I think I saw every episode on *Nick at Nite*. I loved the interplay between the oddball family, especially Morticia and Gomez. In its own way, theirs was a fairy-tale romance."

Jake pivoted and stood. "I can't say I ever thought of it as romantic, but okay. Who was your favorite character?"

Goldie didn't hesitate. "Morticia. You?"

He nodded and grinned. "Morticia." She was hot. He waggled his eyebrows in a Gomez imitation. "Do you speak French?"

"Do you smoke a cigar?" she lobbed back instead, playing off the Morticia/Gomez reference. A hint of a wicked smile that did crazy things to his blood pressure played about her mouth.

"Only when I'm too drunk to know better."

A frown bisected her forehead. "How often is that?"

He supposed that didn't sound so good. He laughed. "Only once in college. A group of buddies, cheap bourbon and even cheaper cigars is a bad combination. I was sick for days." Jake winced and it was Goldie who laughed then, but it held a note of commiseration.

"Been there, done that. Once was enough." She shook her head. "But it was those cheapie mini fast-food burgers instead of cigars. I haven't touched the bourbon or the burgers since."

She moved to stand in front of the fire, holding her hands out in front of her. "The fire feels good."

And quick as a flash, it happened again. One minute they were laughing about *The Addams Family* and bad college bourbon experiences and the next, he was caught up in whatever this was between them. All he could think about was how good she would feel in his arms.

"Considering it's dark, raining and cold, you can forget about finding your clothes tonight." And he needed to forget about anything other than putting some distance between them. "You might as well go back to bed."

"Thanks to you, I can't. When you flipped on that light and yelled, it woke me right up. I couldn't sleep now if my life depended on it."

He could guarantee that his brief glimpse of her breasts

crowned with rosy tips would render him sleepless tonight, as well—and for many nights to come. His entire body tensed at the memory, some parts more tense than others.

"Suit yourself. I'm going to watch TV for a while and get a bite to eat. I'm hungry." Namely for her. It would be in her best interest to go to bed now.

"Let me make you something. It's the least I can do since I ate your wings and drank your beer." There was a teasing note in her voice. He guessed he had sounded a little like an ass when he'd said that.

Jake paused, feeling as if he was balanced at the edge of a precipice. He should tell Goldie to get behind a closed, locked door and not come back out until the light of day when they could locate her clothes and he could haul her back to wherever she wanted to go. Did she have enough sense to know just how damn sexy she looked standing barefoot in front of the fire, wearing his oversize mis-matched duds, her hair tousled from having been asleep in his bed? He damn sure did. Which was why instead of sending her packing, he found himself saying, "That's not necessary. I'm used to fending for myself. But you could keep me company in the kitchen."

She smiled and suddenly, he felt the same sensation he's experienced when he'd wrestled competitively in high school, when he'd found himself pinned to the mat by an opponent. Done for.

4

HANGING OUT WITH JAKE in the kitchen was about the dumbest idea she'd had in, say, a couple of hours, ever since she'd decided to climb naked into his bed. She was bright enough to recognize a flashing caution sign when she saw it.

She *knew* beyond a shadow of a doubt that hightailing it to his bedroom and parking her butt there, with the door closed, until tomorrow morning was the optimal plan. Goldie always rolled with the optimal plan. Except now. Her good sense had picked a heck of a time to play hide-and-seek. But knowing what she should do and doing what she wanted to do had turned out to be two different things.

As dangerous and pointless as it was, she wanted to spend time with Jake. When she was around him, everything inside her felt all tangled up, hot and jangled and wanting, but gloriously alive, nonetheless.

She followed him into the kitchen and perched on one of the stools at the breakfast bar. There was nothing suggestive or sexual in the way Jake leaned into the refrigerator and then emerged with butter, cheese and milk in his hand. Nonetheless, the entire situation was disturbingly, arousingly intimate—the fire, his clothes against her bare flesh, the elemental act of making a meal.

It felt far more like they were two lovers on a weekend

getaway than two business acquaintances temporarily stranded together. Of course that could have a little something to do with the fact that she'd lost herself in those dark eyes of his from the moment she'd first seen him. Even though she'd known she couldn't have him, at least not on her terms.

"Do you want a grilled cheese sandwich and soup?" he said.

She wanted something, but it wasn't that. "Thanks, but I'm fine."

"So, how'd you wind up here at the cottage? You never said earlier." He pulled a can of chunky tomato soup from the cupboard.

While Jake poured the soup and a cup of milk into a saucepan, Goldie told him about her early arrival, her hike, the lack of cell phone service, the tornado warnings and Lauren's invitation to stay at the cabin.

As she rambled, all she could notice were his hands and arms. Good grief, he was fine. His hands were well-shaped, his nails blunt and trimmed. A shiver ran through her at the thought of those hands and his mouth moving against her skin. Dark hair sprinkled his forearms and his biceps bunched distractingly beneath the worn sleeves of his T-shirt as he worked at preparing the meal. She'd noticed it earlier, too, when he built the fire.

Heat spiraled through her, heat that had nothing to do with the crackling logs in the fireplace or the gas stove. This heat was all man-generated. One man in particular. She forced her attention back to the conversation. "Lauren said no one would be here this weekend." It was the Malone brothers' cabin, but he had some explaining to do, as well. "I thought you were out of town on business." Oh, no. That sounded as if she kept up with what he was doing and she most certainly didn't. "I mean, that's why you weren't part of this meeting in the first place." And it was time for her to shut up. She was one sentence, possibly two, away from babbling.

"I was in New York but caught an earlier flight when my meeting was cancelled." The stove sat opposite the breakfast bar and he turned his back to her to put the sandwich in the pan. Goldie'd never been a big fan of a man in sweats, but Jake wore them extremely well. Broad, masculine shoulders, strong arms, sweats riding low on his hips. It was as if he was inviting her to slip her hands beneath the loose edge of his T-shirt and discover whether he actually had chest hair. The very thought made her glad she was sitting. She didn't think her legs would support her.

He turned back around. "Chad told me the cabin was stocked but empty."

On the stove, the buttered bread sizzled against the pan's heat. She knew just how it felt. "I'm sure finding wet clothes on the front porch was a surprise."

He grinned as he flipped the sandwich over. "Not nearly as much of a surprise as when I turned on the light in my bedroom."

...and I found you naked in my bed.

He didn't say it, but it hung there between them. Goldie sat snared by his dark eyes, mesmerized by the desire burning in them, desire that echoed her own want. Speaking of...

"Jake."

"Yes?"

"I think your sandwich is burning."

"Dammit." He flipped it onto the plate and grimaced. "Good thing I like mine well-done." He poured the soup into a bowl and propped himself against the counter, then picked up the sandwich, which was all crispy on the outside but gooey and melted on the inside. Uh-huh. That's exactly how she felt. She knew she was in terrible shape when she started identifying with a grilled cheese sandwich. Pathetic. She shook head. He'd said something but she'd totally missed it because she was so distracted.

"Sorry. What'd you say?"

"I asked if you were still husband hunting?" He bit into the sandwich.

Goldie had the distinct impression he was deliberately goading her. She nodded earnestly, widening her eyes. "Absolutely. I take it you've managed to elude the hordes pursuing you." Sarcasm wasn't a one-way street.

"I'm usually armed with a stick."

"It must be a really big stick." Oh, she was so going where she didn't need to go, but she just couldn't seem to help herself. "You know, crowd control and such."

"It's not so much the size of the stick that's important, but the ability to use it effectively."

She leaned in toward him and lowered her voice conspiratorially. "Sounds like a male myth to me."

He chuckled and washed the last of his sandwich down with a long swallow of beer. Leaning back against the counter in front of the sink, he cocked his head to one side as if studying a specimen. "So, why so desperate to get married? It would be nice to have a little insight into the female psyche."

She wasn't sure whether she wanted to laugh or smack him. Maybe a little bit of both. "I'm not, as you so charmingly put it, desperate. Why are you so scared of commitment?"

He shook his head. "Scared is a poor word choice. Smart enough to avoid is more apt. But you didn't answer my question."

"Why should I discuss that with you?"

"Why not?" His glance slid over her and seemed to say if she could wear his clothes, she could surely answer the question.

"Sure. Okay. I simply don't see the point of wasting my time on men who think like you."

"Ouch." He pretended he'd taken a blow to the gut. Then he straightened and leaned his forearms on the counter, which put him within breathtaking proximity of her. She could literally feel his body heat. Or was that her body heat? Or maybe an intoxicating mix of both? She had no idea because when he was this close, she couldn't think straight. Straight? She wasn't even sure she could think at all. "I can assure you none of my former girlfriends considered dating me a waste of time."

Goldie wasn't given to jealousy. However, the thought of Jake's former girlfriends made her irrationally want to grind her teeth. Instead she smiled sweetly and rallied a brain cell or two, "How fortuitous for you that all women don't think like me."

Outside, rain began to beat on the tin roof once again. A clap of thunder made her jump. Jake's former girlfriends instantly became irrelevant. "It sounds like another thunderstorm rolling in," she said. Was that the sound of hail on the roof? Panic threatened to swamp her. In her experience, hail signaled tornadoes. Still striving for some measure of calm, she slid off the bar stool and headed for the big screen in the den. "I'm going to check out the Weather Channel. If we're going to be blown off the map, I'd like a heads-up."

JAKE WAS FLUMMOXED. One minute they were talking about relationships and the next, Goldie looked as if she'd seen a ghost and was running for the TV. What was her problem? He liked women, but he didn't pretend to even remotely understand them. With no sisters or even close female cousins, he'd never had the inside track on the female mind. He did have a mother, but helping them understand the opposite sex had never been part of her relationship with her sons. Actually, perhaps a greater part of the equation was what had been involved in her relationship with her sons—an ongoing dialogue of pointing out, via the example set by their father, what a man shouldn't do. It was usually coupled with his father's favorite catch-phrase—"What the hell is she going on about now?" In self-defense, Jake had blocked it all out and simply formed the opinion that not having a long-term relationship with a woman was the easiest way to go.

That way a guy didn't have to juggle the one-hundred-plus rules thrown out by his mother and end up clueless like his father. As far as he was concerned, avoidance was the name of the game. He wouldn't end up in a horrible relationship like his parents had and he wouldn't fall short of the mark. Simple enough.

At his own pace, he followed Goldie into the den. She'd settled into Scott's chair and was engrossed in the weather report. Since Jake's chair was temporarily history, he sat in Chad's.

Goldie heaved an audible sigh of relief when the weather anchor announced that thunderstorms were rolling through and there was still flash flooding, but the cabin wasn't in the list of counties under tornado warning. Her smile was shaky. "Yay. We're not going to get sucked up by a tornado tonight. We're not going to die."

Jake slanted a look her way. "You were seriously worried about it?"

"Of course. Otherwise I wouldn't have had those beers earlier. I just wanted to be buzzed when the time came."

She had the strangest sense of humor. But it was kind of funny. He laughed. "So, you thought you might die and you wanted to die drunk?"

"Go ahead and laugh. Isn't there anything you're afraid of?"

Crap. She wasn't being funny. She was serious. She'd really been afraid. He reached across, spanning the distance between their chairs, and caught her hand up in his, offering solace, reassurance and a measure of apology. "Hey, it's okay. I'm sorry I laughed. I didn't realize you were really afraid."

For a second he thought she was going to pull her hand away from his, but he felt the instant she decided not to withdraw. An odd sense of relief washed over him. "I can handle spiders, snakes, the dark, but tornadoes do me in." Her fingers curled around his.

He rubbed the back of her hand with his thumb. "Then we're in luck. The tornadoes have bypassed us tonight." He paused. "Failure."

"What?"

"You asked me if I was afraid of anything. Failure. I'm afraid of failing, of letting people down." Well, damn. He'd never actually said that to anyone else. He wasn't sure that he'd actually ever realized it before. And it should be frightening to offer her an inside glimpse of the man he was, but in front of the fire, with the TV on in the background, it seemed the most natural thing to do, to reveal himself to this woman. "I think it comes from being the last in a long line of overachievers."

She nodded slowly. This time, she was the one plying her thumb on the back of his hand in a soothing motion. "One of my college professors always told us that without failure we would never realize our true potential."

"Easier said than done."

"That's true of anything. You need to cut yourself some slack. I'm sure Chad has made some bad business decisions. Surely Scott doesn't win every sporting event he enters."

"I guess I never really thought of it that way." Living up to his older brothers had always seemed a mountain to be scaled, a point to be proven. That was one reason he was so damned proud of the job he did in the sales department. He was kicking butt and taking names in his job. "What about you? Do you have any brothers or sisters?"

She tucked her feet beneath her to one side. "Nope. I'm an only only."

That was an odd term. "An only child?"

"Yep. An only child with only one parent."

He hazarded a guess. "Your mother?"

"Right in one. My parents were never married and when my mother got pregnant, my father skipped. He didn't think he was parent material."

Jake was at a momentary loss for words. That explained a whole helluva lot about Goldie Dawkins right there. And he knew exactly where she was coming from, even though he was on the flip side of the proverbial coin. "I'm not saying you're lucky because…well, that would be presumptuous. But if it's any consolation, my parents fought constantly. The classic case of staying together for the kids' sake. In fact, they still fight constantly. Family holidays are hell."

"They're still together?"

"Yeah. I think they've grown so used to making one another miserable, they don't know what else to do."

Goldie smiled, but there was a tinge of melancholy about it. "I…uh…saw their picture." She nodded her head toward the Grand Canyon photo in the corner.

"They almost look normal and happy there, which is why Scott has it on the wall. He likes to pretend there's nothing wrong with their relationship." Jake shook his head. He'd given up trying to figure it out. "At some point they must've liked one another well enough to have three kids, but I can't recall them ever getting along."

"And that is precisely why I'm going to try very hard to get it right when I choose a mate," she said.

"And that is precisely why temporary mates are a beautiful thing," he countered. "You make a mistake and none of the parties involved suffer any long-term consequences."

A small frown crossed her face as she seriously weighed his comment. For some weird reason, she struck him as incredibly beautiful at that moment. She shook her head. "No. I want what I didn't have growing up."

He took up his position on the opposite side of the fence. "So do I."

Whatever she might've said was lost when, in rapid succession, it thundered, lightning flashed and the cabin was suddenly plunged into darkness except for the flickering, dying firelight.

What happened next, Jake wasn't exactly sure. He and Goldie jumped up out of their recliners at the same time. Whether she tripped or he bumped into her he didn't know. One second they were upright and the next, they were on the floor on the braided rug, with all of Goldie's soft womanly curves beneath him.

ALL THE BREATH WHOOSHED out of her.

"Are you okay?" Jake asked, his breath feathering against her face.

"No," she said without thinking. She'd never, ever be okay again, now that she knew just how good it felt to have him on top of her. Her resolve fractured and weakened beneath the weight of his hips against hers.

"What hurts?" he asked, concern evident in his voice.

Well, hell. Now she had to make something up to cover. "I landed awkwardly on my hip."

He shifted against her and, dear God, it was all she could do not to grind her hips up against him. "Which hip?"

"My left," she lied through her teeth. "But it's fine now."

"Here?" Oh. My. God. His broad hand smoothing over her hip bone, even through the cotton pants, left a trail of fire in its wake.

"Uh-huh." It was all she was capable of uttering.

Jake began making small circular massage motions. "Is that better?" He sounded winded, short of breath, which was precisely the way she felt.

"Much." And it would be better still if he'd just move that motion around to the front, right to that hot, hard ache between her thighs. All rational thought disappeared. She reached up and wrapped her arms around his neck, weaving her fingers through his hair, stroking his skin.

His harsh intake of breath was almost as arousing as his touch.

"But now I seem to have developed a different kind of ache altogether," she said.

He lowered his head until his lips were warm and firm against the corner of her mouth. "Tell me I shouldn't kiss you. Tell me this is a bad idea."

"You shouldn't kiss me," she said quite insincerely, since she wanted nothing more at that moment than to have his lips against hers. "It's a seriously bad idea."

His lips feathered over hers, the gossamer touch of butterfly wings that left her with a deep ache for more.

"Beyond seriously bad," he said.

"Uh-huh," she uttered, her breath mingling with his, her whole body singing at the scrape of his five o'clock shadow against her cheek. Jake deepened the kiss and simultaneously she seemed to melt into the rug and press upward against him.

And then the kisses became slow, drugging touches that were almost pure magic. Goldie liked to kiss and Jake was a good kisser—make that a great kisser. Some guys were sloppy, some wet, some perfunctory, some rushed as if swapping some spit was nothing more than a prerequisite for the final act. Kissing Jake, on the other hand, was sublime.

Somewhere along the line, they'd rolled onto their sides to face one another and he caressed her beneath the T-shirt. She dragged her toe up his sweatpant-clad leg.

He pulled away from her mouth and immediately found the underside of her jaw and her neck with his beautiful, talented lips. A tremor shook her and she moaned low and deep in her throat.

"Goldie…" His eyes were fathomless in the shadows cast by the firelight. He sat up and scrubbed his hand over his head. "I'm sorry. I didn't mean for that to happen. It shouldn't have happened. It won't happen again."

Shaken, Goldie sat up and tugged her T-shirt and sweat-shirt, well, *his* duds back down over her thighs. Thank God one of them had shown some sense. Unfortunately it hadn't been her. If it'd been up to her, she'd still be rolling around on the rug making out with the last man she ought to be making out with.

How embarrassing that he'd been the one to call a halt. While her pump was more than primed and ready to go, he obviously found her utterly resistible.

"I'll just head to bed now," she said. For good measure she tacked on, "Alone." Just so he'd know he wasn't the only one who wanted to stop.

He stood and extended his hand to help her up. "That's an excellent idea."

She ignored his hand, not to be bitchy but simply because she didn't trust herself not to fling herself on top of him if she touched him again. She was skating that close to the edge of insanity. She moved toward the hallway, eager to put some distance between them. "Good night." She strove for a casual smile.

"Can you find your way in the dark?"

"I'll manage. Thanks."

She had known he was the brother to avoid. Now that she knew how dangerous he was, she was determined not to touch Jake Malone again with that ten-foot pole. And this time she meant it.

SONOFABITCH. THIS WAS precisely why he had avoided Goldie Dawkins. He'd kissed his fair share of women. No doubt about it, some were better than others. But kissing Goldie had been incredible. And touching her had been incredible. The feel of her skin, the taste of her mouth, the sheer rightness of the two of them being together... It made no sense given their diametrically opposed views on relationships, but still, it was there.

He scrubbed his hand through his hair, very much aware of the arousal he currently sported. Stopping had damn near killed him. While no one could accuse him of leading her on or making promises he didn't intend to keep, he wouldn't take advantage of her and the situation.

He stirred the fire, rousing sparks, and threw on another log. If he was honest, the staring-him-in-the-face truth of the matter was that he'd called a halt to the fun and games because she scared him. She shook him up. He felt more raw intense emotion, just in rolling around on the floor with her sharing a couple of kisses than he had making love to most women.

If it wasn't the dead of night and the middle of a thunderstorm, he'd go out and chop some wood to vent his frustration. Unfortunately, it was both storming and close to midnight. Which left him with the option of—

Crash. This time, it wasn't the boom of thunder. The noise came from his bedroom. Low, intense swearing immediately followed.

"You okay?" he yelled, sprinting down the dark, short hall.

"I'm fine, but stop at the doorway," Goldie said with a catch in her voice. What the…? It wasn't as if he wasn't going to be able to contain himself. "I just knocked the lamp off the bedside table," she continued. "Therc's glass on the floor."

Jake stopped in the doorway. The fire's glow from the den did nothing to illuminate the dark bedroom. "You're a one-woman wrecking crew."

"I try."

"Sorry." Okay, he'd sounded like a jerk but actually the lamp was the least of his worries. She was wrecking *him*.

"I'll clean it up," she said. "If you'll get me a flashlight and a broom."

"Not barefooted, you won't." Yes, he'd noticed her bare feet. They were sort of long and narrow and her toenails had been painted a deep, dark red that had contrasted erotically with her white, white skin. "I'll grab my shoes and a flashlight. Just stay put."

Within a minute, he was back with the trash can, a broom and flashlight, his own feet shoved into his sodden shoes. His gut tightened and his willpower nosedived at the sight of her sitting in his bed, even though the covers were modestly pulled up to her chin and she was fully dressed.

It didn't make a damn bit of difference—because the image of seeing her there naked was forever burned into his brain.

He stopped at the foot of the bed. "Put this on the nightstand, if you would," he said. The flashlight was really more of a battery-operated lantern.

"Sure."

His fingers brushed hers in the figurative passing of the torch and he could've sworn there was a spark. The electricity might be out in the cabin, but there was plenty being generated between the two of them.

5

GOLDIE SCOOTED TO THE middle of the bed, desperate to put as much distance as possible between her and Jake in the small bedroom. He wielded the broom with the same efficiency he'd shown in everything else he'd done—including kissing her nearly senseless.

"I think that's got it," he said. However, the sharp crunch of glass underfoot as he stepped forward announced otherwise. Jake swore. "It's going to be impossible to get this all up without better light and a mop. You can't sleep in here because it's not safe for you to cross the room without shoes."

Much as she hated to say it, he was right. "Okay. That makes sense."

He propped the broom and dustpan against the wall and crossed to the edge of the bed. "I'll carry you out."

She swallowed hard and repeated stupidly, "Carry me out?"

"You don't want to pick up a piece of glass in your foot." She wanted to protest, to refuse, because she really, really didn't want the sweet temptation of being back in his arms, of sharing body heat and chemistry, but there was no way to refuse without looking irrational.

A sudden horrifying thought hit her. Forget sweet temptation. How about abject humiliation? She was no petite, diminutive little thing. What if he staggered beneath her weight? "I'm not sure you can carry me—"

"For Pete's sake," he interrupted her, taking her by surprise and scooping her up. Instinctively she looped her arms around his neck, holding on, putting his jaw and the strong column of his neck within tantalizing, kissable proximity.

"Are you good?" he asked, his breath warm against her cheek. Her heart thudded like a mad thing in her chest.

"I'm fine," she managed to say. It was both heaven and hell to be cradled against his chest. His hair teased against her wrists and fingers. His scent, a combination of his cologne, soap and man, wrapped around her. For a brief second she gave into temptation and rested her head against his shoulder.

He crossed the room, taking care to angle through the doorway so as not to bump her feet on the doorjamb. He stopped midway down the hall. "This should be safe."

She wanted to laugh hysterically, as if anything within shouting distance of him was safe. Right. "Thanks."

He released her legs and she slid down his front. However, his arm remained wrapped around her shoulders and she still had her hands linked behind his neck.

With a harsh intake of breath and a low, heated, *"Cara mia,"* Jake pulled her more firmly to him and nuzzled her temple. Gomez to Morticia.

Without thinking, she nibbled at the spot between his ear and jaw. She felt him shudder beneath her lips. She gave up, gave in. She was tired of fighting her attraction to him. *"Voulez vous coucher avec moi ce soir?"* Morticia to Gomez. Loosely, *would you like to sleep with me tonight?*

He leaned into her, pressing her against the wall, and feathered kisses over her temple, down her cheek. "Are you sure, Goldie?" Why couldn't he just shut up and let her lose herself in the magic of the moment? He smoothed his thumb over the angle of her cheek. "I'm the same man... I can't make any promises...."

No, he wouldn't make promises. He was a man of honor. He'd been straightforward with her from the beginning. But for him to give her an out, a chance to say no when she could feel the hard press of his erection at the juncture of her thighs—most men would simply run with the opportunity. But then again, Jake Malone wasn't most men. She knew he couldn't offer her what she wanted long-term, but for tonight he'd be hers.

"I'm sure," she said, canting her hips against his in blatant invitation.

He groaned and swooped in for a kiss, his mouth hot and demanding, their tongues tangling impatiently. He tasted good and felt even better. She moaned into his mouth and they strained against one another. She slid her hands beneath his shirt and explored his back. Velvet skin over well-formed muscles. He cupped her breast through the layers of T-shirt and sweatshirt and she ached for more. He dragged his mouth from hers, his breathing ragged.

"Wrap your arms around my neck again," he said.

"Why?"

"Because, Ms. Dawkins—" he slowly traced a circle around her nipple with his index finger "—we're going to slow this down. I've waited too damn long for you to rush this now." Yes! He'd wanted her from the beginning, too. He brushed his finger over her hardened point and it was like a direct line from her breast to the slick heat between her thighs. Was he trying to make her crazy? He was doing a good job. "I'm going to carry you back into my room—"

"But the glass." She still had a little sense left.

He cupped her breast in his hand. "I guess we'll both have to stay there. Because I'm not going to make love to you in one of my brothers' beds. I want you in mine."

Well, then. If he kept touching her like this and saying things like that, he could have her right here in the hall if he wanted to. But the bed probably was a better idea.

She wrapped her hands around his neck again. "Ready when you are."

JAKE SHOULDERED BACK through his bedroom door. There was no way in hell she was sleeping anywhere but his bed tonight. He'd wanted her from day one. God help him, he'd tried, he'd really tried. He'd made sure he was out of the office on days she was scheduled to come in. He'd tried to stay away tonight and he couldn't.

Her head against his shoulder, she laughed softly. "I guess I can say you walked across broken glass for me."

"Twice." Jake smiled at her whimsy. That was part of her charm—the mixture of practical businesswoman and romantic. He might not be capable of giving her what she wanted long-term, but tonight he'd offer her everything he had.

He settled her on the bed and then stood back to look. "You are beautiful," he said. And she was.

"You are obviously delusional, but thank you." She glanced at the lantern on the nightstand. "You can turn that off."

"I will if you want me to, but I'd really, really like to see you naked." Whoa. Maybe that sounded a little crass. "I mean, I've thought about you naked a lot—" Way to go, hoss. That was way better than *I'd like to see you naked.* Now he sounded like a pervert.

"You have?"

She didn't sound or look offended. Actually, she looked kind of pleased. And since confession was reportedly good for the soul… "Yeah. I have. Numerous times."

"Oh, good. Me, too."

"You've thought about me naked?"

She settled back on her elbows and the expression in her eyes sent his dick into warp mode. "More times than I can count."

Well damn. That was both arousing and intimidating. She'd mentioned a big stick earlier. He was comfortable with his stick but what if it wasn't as big as she'd imagined? "I can turn the lantern off."

She looked up at him and the courage and trust in her eyes stole his breath away. "I'm not a Playboy centerfold—"

"Honey, I'm no male porn star."

She smiled. "I'm willing to leave it on if you are."

"On it is." And then, because he figured she'd be less self-conscious if he got naked first, he pulled his T-shirt off.

"Oh." She sat up.

"Oh?" She hadn't sounded disappointed.

With a sly smile, she knelt on the mattress. She reached out and trailed her finger along his skin. "I like your chest hair."

"I'm glad." That *was* a relief. Men without body hair seemed to be in vogue these days and that wasn't him.

"Not nearly as glad as I am." Goldie leaned forward and scattered a series of quick kisses over his chest, ending with a wicked swipe of her pink tongue across one of his flat, male nipples. A fireball rushed through him. He hooked his thumbs in his sweats and pulled them down and off.

"Oh. My." There was no mistaking the appreciation in her blue eyes.

He smiled and reached for her. "I take it you approve."

"Definitely."

He settled on the bed, propping himself on one arm. "Then for God's sake, woman, put me out of my misery."

"Misery?"

He grinned. "I will be in absolute, utter misery until I see you naked again."

Her smile teased as she pulled his sweatshirt over her head and off. "Better?"

Her nipples thrust against the T-shirt in rigid attention. "We're getting there."

She reached beneath the hem of the shirt and shimmied the pajama bottoms down and off, leaving her legs bare but her upper thighs and torso covered. Her legs were slender, yet toned. In about two seconds, or less, he mentally had them wrapped around his waist.

"Come here," he said. "You're like the Christmas present I've been waiting to open since before Thanksgiving." He settled back against the headboard and tugged her to him. On her knees, she straddled his thighs.

There was a nervous, shy edge to her smile. "Then I guess it's Christmas in May. Unwrap me."

His hands weren't quite steady as he caught the hem of the T-shirt and tugged it up and off her. For a second, time stood still. Goldie wasn't just another naked woman in his bed. She was the embodiment of womanhood, and she was his...at least for tonight. Full, round, rose-tipped breasts, smooth alabaster skin, and at the juncture of her thighs, a trim dark triangle of curls. He forced himself to breathe. "You are absolutely perfect."

No man had ever looked at her the way Jake did. A heady combination of lust and reverence shone in his eyes. And for that moment, she felt perfect.

He pulled her down to the mattress to lie beside him. He looked at her from head to toe, his glance leaving a trail of fire in its wake. He cradled her head in his big hand, his eyes fathomless. She smoothed her hands over his muscled shoulders, reveling in the feel of him beneath her fingertips. Everything else faded to nothing as her senses became focused on the two of them.

It became a mutual exploration of one another. With his mouth, his touch, his whispered words, he wooed her.

"I've waited so long to do this," he said, scattering kisses down her neck, across her collarbone, until he reached her breasts. Her heart raced and she buried her hands in his hair, gasping as he flicked his tongue against her nipple. First one and then the other, winding her spring of wanting inside her tighter and tighter.

"And this…" While he licked and sucked her sensitive nipples, he skimmed his hand over her belly and the curve of her hip. Her muscles clenched in anticipation of his touch. He stroked her inner thigh and ran his fingers along her skin, almost but not quite touching her where she ached to be touched. Finally, he dipped his finger into her wet slickness.

"Yes, oh, yes." She almost didn't recognize her own voice.

She reached between them and stroked the length of him. He was all ridged velvet stretched taut. She loved the feel of his heat, his hardness against her palm and fingers. He moaned and pulsed beneath her touch. She stroked up him, catching a small pearl of moisture on the tip of her finger, then smoothed it back down his length.

Finally, it was no longer enough to touch and be touched. She didn't just *want* him inside her, she *needed* him inside her as desperately as she needed her next breath.

"Do you have—"

"Yes."

It could've been awkward as he retrieved a condom from the nightstand and rolled it on, but it wasn't. It was simply the next step in the journey they were taking together.

They both gasped in pleasure as he entered her. She was tight and wet and he was just the right size to stretch her and fill her. Fully in her, he paused and she pulsed around him. "Oh, honey…"

"I know," she said. It was as if they were custom-made for one another. And it wasn't only physically—it was as if they were tuned into what each other wanted and how they wanted it.

With each stroke, they shared a give-and-take, gaining momentum. Everything became distilled to just the two of them. The need for release, the need to give pleasure. When her orgasm rolled through her it was unlike anything she'd experienced before. Jake took her and went with her to a new place. It was a place she never wanted to leave.

"MORNING."

Goldie blinked, momentarily disoriented. Oh, yeah, Jake's bed, Jake's cabin, mind-boggling sex a couple of times in the night. She was with the program pronto.

"Morning." For about one millisecond she considered being embarrassed about what had happened last night, but she equally quickly dismissed the silly notion. They were both adults and they'd both had a good time. A *very* good time.

And there were more pressing issues. She needed to brush her teeth. She wasn't about to risk turning off the sexiest, most interesting man she'd ever found herself in bed with when halitosis was an easily addressed issue. "Is there a spare toothbrush in the bathroom?"

He grinned and nodded. "Let me pull on my jeans and shoes and I'll give you a piggyback ride over to see."

"A naked piggyback ride?"

"It sounds like just the way to start the day." The way he looked at her changed her insides to mush. "I may never clean that glass up."

Goldie liked the fact that there was no awkwardness, no self-consciousness between them. She watched him rise from the bed sporting an early morning hard-on. He certainly had a nice package. Not so big a woman wanted to beg her partner to keep that thing away from her and not so small that she wondered if it was in. She'd definitely known it was in.

And the rest of him was more than easy on the eyes. Well-shaped, muscular legs, an extremely nice male derriere, trim waist, and once again she exalted in the hair on his chest. That was nice—very nice. What the heck, it was all nice.

He pulled on his jeans and shot her an amused glance. "You through looking?"

Totally unabashed, she smiled back at him. "For now."

"Then climb on, babe."

Hmm. They'd seen one another naked but that had been in lantern light. This was different. He was about to see her in all her bare splendor. She hesitated. Her thighs could be tighter, her belly flatter and her breasts definitely perkier. Then again, he'd liked it all well enough last night. She threw off her self-consciousness along with the covers. The flicker in his eyes said he didn't see a thing wrong with what he was looking at. Good nonverbal response.

"Are you through looking?" she asked.

"Not by a long shot. But if you don't get on now, you can forget about brushing your teeth."

Yes. That was precisely the thing to say. She started to roll to her knees and her body put up a screaming protest.

Jake noticed her hesitation. "You okay?"

"Fine." The best cure for a sore muscle group was another workout, which was precisely what she had in mind.

She climbed on his back and he didn't even try to hide his groan. "It's definitely decided. I'm not cleaning up the glass…and I forbid you to, either."

She wrapped her legs around his waist, pressing her mound against his bare back, and wrapped her arms around his neck.

"You *forbid* me?" She flicked her tongue against the skin right behind his ear and rubbed her nipples against his back.

"Goldie, you keep that up and we're definitely not going to make it into the bathroom."

She laughed, loving the way he made her feel, as if she was the sexiest woman on the planet and he couldn't keep his hands off her. "I'll behave."

"Well, don't behave too much." He skimmed the back of her calf with his hand.

"Count on it…as soon as I've brushed my teeth."

Chuckling, Jake made quick work of carrying her to the bathroom. Riding piggyback naked was a decidedly erotic experience—one she could get used to with him. Who was she kidding? She could get used to a lot of things with him…only now wasn't the time or place to think such crazy thoughts.

He deposited her at the bathroom door. "I'm not much of a cook, but are you hungry?"

It was kind of embarrassing to admit, because she obviously had plenty of flesh on her bones, but she was ravenous. Good sex could work up quite the appetite. "I am. But give me a minute—and a T-shirt—and I'll cook."

His grin stole her breath. "That's a deal. There's a package of spare toothbrushes in the cabinet under the sink. Chad's anal about that kind of thing." He would be. "Help yourself."

Once she closed the door behind Jake, Goldie glanced in the mirror and then wished she hadn't. Ouch. Her hair looked as if it'd been put through a blender. Good God almighty. But Jake hadn't seemed to notice or if he had noticed, he hadn't seemed to care. She certainly hadn't caught any expressions of horror on his face. Quite the contrary.

She found a fresh toothbrush and took care of that, also

finding mouthwash and gargling for good measure. She finger combed her hair and washed her face. Opening the bathroom door, she discovered a T-shirt folded neatly on the floor outside, which she promptly donned.

A quick glance in the bedroom showed he'd cleaned up the lamp debris while she'd been in the bathroom. She found Jake in the den.

"The power's still out," he said, "and until the rain stops and the water subsides, I'm sure Rotter's Creek is impassable. We're stuck here until we can cross the creek."

"Oh."

"The good news is we've got a gas stove, so we can still eat."

Correction, she thought, the good news was that they were stuck. He might be forbidden fruit, but if a girl was stuck, a girl was stuck. She had to take the necessary means to amuse herself.

"What about the hot water heater? Gas or electric?" She could use a shower.

"Unfortunately, electric. But it should still have about a shower's worth stored in it."

"It's all doable." But mostly he was doable. "How about we eat first?"

"I thought you'd never ask."

She laughed and shook her head. "Typical man."

Goldie had seen eggs in the fridge the night before. She took quick stock of the cabinets. Beans, an unopened jar of salsa. This could work. She turned to Jake, who stood propped in the doorway, silently watching as if he was perfectly content to check her out checking his cabinets' contents out. "How about huevos rancheros?"

"You can do that?"

"I can do that."

"You're a goddess."

Goldie laughed and nodded. How was it being with him was so easy? "Of course I am."

She pulled all the ingredients out of the cabinet and he straightened from where he'd stood propped in the doorway. "Want me to open those?"

"I thought you said you were lousy in the kitchen."

"I said I couldn't cook very well. But I open a mean can."

"Open away, then."

In the meantime, she took eggs and preshredded cheese out of the refrigerator and then dug a large skillet and lid out of the cabinet. Within minutes she'd dumped out the cans, cracked a few eggs—two for him, one for her—and had breakfast simmering on the stove.

"Wow. I didn't want to distract you before, but now..." He wrapped his arms around her from behind and nuzzled at her neck, sending a rash of shivers coursing through her.

She was caught between the counter and him and there was definitely a growing ridge pressing against her buttocks. "You think that might distract me?" She wiggled against him.

"Maybe." Jake reached around and cupped her breasts in his hands, catching each nipple between his thumb and forefinger, tugging. "Or this might."

She dropped her head back to his shoulder and pushed her chest harder into his hands. "It's a definite possibility."

"How long do the eggs take?"

"About another three minutes."

"I think we both need a little longer than that."

"I think you're right. Why don't you grab two plates and some silverware?"

"I like what I'm holding on to better, but in the interest of eating in three minutes..."

Jake made her laugh. He was a rare mix of seriously sexy with a great sense of humor. So often seriously sexy, seriously handsome men took themselves...well, too seriously. Jake seemed to be an exception, although he had the handsome, sexy part down pat.

He let go of her breasts, which he couldn't possibly regret more than she did, and then surprised her by slapping her on the bare butt. "Serve me my breakfast."

"If you don't watch it, you'll be wearing your breakfast," she shot back without rancor, in the same teasing vein.

A few minutes later they were seated at the breakfast bar. Jake was eating as if she'd put a gourmet meal before him instead of what she'd cobbed together from the cupboard.

"So, what'd you think of the hike up here yesterday?" he said as he tucked into the eggs and beans.

"The first part was great, right up until it started to pour. After that, I knew I was going to arrive for the business meeting looking like a drowned rat."

He smirked at that. "I bet you'll check the weather next time." She wrinkled her nose at him and he laughed. "There are some great hiking trails up here. If the rain stops we could check them out...if you want to. I usually take my camera along but it's being repaired."

"I'd love to. But if we actually find my shoes, they're going to be soaking wet."

"Damn. I hadn't thought about that. Crazy raccoon." He glanced down at her feet. "What size shoe do you wear?"

"Nine or nine and a half, depending on the brand and cut. Why, do you have a closet of spares?" She couldn't help but wonder, quite unhappily, if he kept various sizes for the different women he brought up to the cabin.

"Hardly, but we may be in luck." He hopped up. "I'll be right back." He disappeared down the hall.

Goldie peered around the corner, noting that he went into Scott's room rather than his own.

He returned in a few minutes, a pair of low-cut hikers in hand. "Today's our lucky day. Size nine and a half. One of Scott's former girlfriends left them behind. They sat in the den for a month before he finally tossed them into the back of his closet."

"Does that ever get awkward?"

"What?"

"Bringing girlfriends up here. Do you each take rotating weekends or how do you work that?" She strove for a neutral tone but inside, she had a sick feeling in the pit of her stomach at the thought of the women who had sat where she was sitting now, having a morning-after breakfast with Jake. And that was just silly. She had no proprietary interests in Jake Malone.

He picked up his fork, shrugging. "It's never been an issue. Sheila's the only woman Scott ever brought and they were damn near engaged. Chad occasionally plans a working weekend like the one he'd set up for Friday." His eyes held hers. "I've never brought anyone here."

His answer left her ridiculously, dangerously relieved. It shouldn't matter one whit to her whether he kept an entire harem on the property. It shouldn't, but it did. "And now I've invaded your space."

His voice was low and soft. "Do you hear me complaining?"

Yet another response that set her foolish heart singing. "Those are your photos in the den?"

"Yeah. They're mine. I love it up here and I like capturing it with my camera."

And somehow what should've been a fifteen-minute breakfast turned into an hour and a half. They discussed hiking and photography, travel, movies and the wine business. He was smart and funny and a good conversationalist. Her last boyfriend had been fond of his own voice, for sure. Not that Jake was her boyfriend. He was just…well, a mistake she fully planned to get out of her system in the next day or so.

Together they stacked the dishes in the sink. "Let's not waste water on the dishes," he said, once again trapping her against the counter and nuzzling her neck. "Since there's only enough hot water for one shower, I suggest in the interests of conservation that we shower together." He slid his hands up beneath her T-shirt and stroked the already-wet channel between her thighs. "I can get any of those hard-to-reach places for you."

She rocked against his questing fingers. "I am all about conservation…and a useful man."

7

"THAT WAS A BAD IDEA," Goldie said, but she was laughing. Jake wrapped a towel around her and then snagged his own. She had beautiful eyes. Her lashes were long but a light brown.

"You were all for showering together," he said.

"Yeah, but we wouldn't have run out of hot water if we'd stuck to just showering."

He blotted a wet spot on her shoulder with the end of his towel. "I had no idea how easily distracted you were."

She sputtered in mock outrage. "Me? I think you're talking about yourself, mister." One side of her towel dropped, revealing the smooth globe of her left breast.

He could look at her naked body all day, any day. And he was never ever going to see her again at the office without thinking of her this way. Those would be hard times, in more than one way. Knotting his towel about his waist, he leaned against the doorjamb. "I have to say, that's pretty distracting."

Goldie yanked her towel back up into place with a smile. Glancing over at him, she hesitated, her glance sweeping over him, lingering on his bare chest and belly, the low-slung towel. "You're pretty distracting yourself." Her voice had taken on a husky quality.

As gratifying as it was to have her look at him that way,

he wasn't superstud. His business wouldn't be good to go again for another little while. "I'm curious about something," he said.

"Yes?" She stood in front of the bathroom mirror finger combing her short blond hair into place.

"Goldie's an unusual name. Is it a family name?"

"Nothing so sentimental. And it's not short for anything like Golda or Goldina. My mother always liked Goldie Hawn so I was Goldie from the day she found out she was having a girl." She pulled the T-shirt she'd worn earlier over her head. The towel dropped out from below. "When I was a kid, I hated it. I hated it all the way through high school. Kids just want to fit in." She shrugged, hanging the towel on a wall hook. "But I like it now. I certainly don't run into other people very often with the same name."

"It suits you. You're unique." And she was. He'd never met anyone else quite like her. And it wasn't one single thing he could put his finger on—it was just *her.*

She planted her hands on her hips, humor glinting in her eyes. "Are you saying I'm weird?"

Jake laughed. It was nice to be around a woman who was both sexy and possessed a sense of humor. Not to mention she hadn't complained even once about the lack of electricity. And the sex had zoomed to the top of his Best Sex I Ever Had list. Plus, she could carry on an intelligent conversation. Most beautiful women weren't as interesting as Goldie Dawkins. And last, but not least, she seemed to get him. Excepting her matrimony requirement fatal flaw, she was the perfect woman.

He bridged the space separating them and pulled her close to him. He couldn't get it up so shortly after their shower bout, but he could at least hold her close. "By no stretch of imagination did I call you weird. Unique is good, weird is weird."

She smiled and linked her arms around his neck, "I'd say you're pretty unique yourself."

"I am?"

Laughing, Goldie pressed a kiss to his lips. "You are." She leaned back in his arms and cocked her head to one side. "Do you hear that?"

"Hear what?"

"The rain's stopped."

She was right. There was no patter against the cabin's tin roof. "So it has."

"Maybe we can track down Fester's hiding place and snag my clothes."

"Let me get dressed and I can do that."

She looked down at the too-big T-shirt she was wearing. "Did Sheila happen to leave any clothes behind?"

They headed into his bedroom together.

"Sorry. Only the shoes." Not that he was really sorry. He liked seeing her wear his T-shirt, almost as much as he liked seeing her wearing nothing at all. He smiled at the thought.

"What's so funny?" she said.

"Nothing really." He pulled on a pair of clean underwear and blue jeans.

"Uh-huh." She picked his pajama pants off the foot of the bed where they'd wound up last night and stepped into them.

What the hell? If she really wanted to know.... "I was just thinking that I like seeing you wear my T-shirt, almost as much as I like seeing you wearing nothing at all. You wear nothing well."

"Oh." A hint of color crept up her face as she pulled the drawstring waist tight and secured it. She eyed his bare chest and unzipped jeans. "It's a good look on you, too."

All she had to do was glance at him that way and he wanted

her all over again. "If you don't quit shooting me those looks, we're not going to make it outside until much later."

She laughed. "Then you'd better put on a shirt because the scenery is nice from where I'm standing."

Tugging a T-shirt over his head, he couldn't help but grin. "Better?"

"In the interest of finding my clothes, I guess so."

As he'd told her earlier, he'd never brought a girlfriend to the cabin. It had always been a private retreat he'd never cared to share. Even though he hadn't brought Goldie here either, he realized he wanted to show her the surrounding area. He had a feeling she'd appreciate the peace and beauty. There was, however, one thing she needed to know up front. "You know, there's no guarantee we'll find all of your clothes. And there's no telling what state they'll be in." He tossed her a pair of socks. "You'll need these for the shoes."

"Thanks." Perching on the mattress's edge, she put them on and pulled on his hoodie. "Okay, let's go round up my clothes."

She should've looked ridiculous. Instead she was incredibly sexy and inspiring. She made him want to slay dragons or some other equally ridiculous heroic feat just to look good in her eyes. And that was just plain misguided. Because despite the great sex they'd shared, they both knew he was the wrong man for her.

GOLDIE STARED AT THE sodden mess that was her clothes. They'd found them in the second place Jake had checked.

"Wow, I didn't think Fester would have washed, dried and folded them, but I didn't expect this either."

Jake sent her a sympathetic look. "He's a wild animal with sharp teeth and claws."

She really hadn't spent a whole lot of time thinking about her clothes—she'd been too busy with Jake—but now she considered the implications of having her clothes stolen by a raccoon. "Do you think he might've…well… marked them? Do raccoons do that?"

"I'm no expert, but probably."

Ew. She picked up a stick and lifted her T-shirt. There was a rip down the front and it was covered in dirt and leaves. Her panties were beneath the T-shirt. Even without picking them up with the stick, she could see that the crotch had been gnawed through. "Well."

Jake chuckled from behind her. "Fester's a raccoon of discriminating taste."

"Very funny. Those were my favorite panties."

"Apparently he liked them, too. Sorry. I couldn't help myself." He sobered. "Do you want me to take them to the cabin?"

"Even if I washed them several times, I don't think I'd ever feel comfortable wearing any of them when I think of that marking business." She dropped the T-shirt back onto the pile and tossed the stick to the ground. "I'll have to borrow your clothes to get home."

"Not a problem. It's the least I can do since Fester destroyed yours. I guess it really isn't funny, is it?"

"Actually, it is, sort of. I can't say I've ever had my clothes stolen by a raccoon before. And I've learned an important life lesson—never leave your wet clothes on the front porch in the middle of the woods." She shrugged it off with a laugh. "So, how about that hike you were talking about?"

"There's a clearing northeast of here. You can see for miles from there."

"I'm following you."

They set off and a comfortable silence developed

between them. On a steep part of the trail, several times he turned around and offered her a helping hand. At one point he stopped, his fingers against his lips in a quieting motion, and pointed through the trees. A white-tailed doe and her fawn stood grazing in a thicket. The wind shifted and the mother looked up, startled. Quick as a flash, they were gone.

Goldie realized she'd been holding her breath. "That was awesome."

"It was, wasn't it?" The trail had widened and Jake reached out and caught her hand in his. "This was part of an old logging road. We're almost there. Just a little bit further."

It felt so right, so achingly romantic to walk through the woods together holding hands. A few yards up the trail, Jake led them past the trees to an outcropping of rocks. "Watch your step and don't get too close to the edge. The rocks will be a little slippery from the rain. Hold on a sec."

He released her hand and climbed up to a particularly large boulder. Leaning back down to her, he extended his hands. "Here, I'll help you up."

Within seconds, she was on top of the boulder with him. A vista of rounded mountains, some of the oldest in the United States, was spread before them. Brooding thunderclouds loomed in the distance. He wrapped his arms around her from behind, his solid warmth at her back, his cheek against her hair.

"It's beautiful," she said, moved by both the mountains and the man.

"I knew you would like it," he said, his breath warming her cheek as he tightened his arms about her.

"I love it." *And I love you.*

For one heart-stopping moment, she was afraid she'd spoken the words aloud. How had this happened? She wasn't prone to fancying herself in love. In fact, while she'd really liked Brett, she'd never felt this way before. Then again, she'd felt something from the very first moment she'd met Jake. It was as if she'd found what she'd been looking for, but didn't want to acknowledge it. She'd run; she'd kept her distance until this weekend had made that impossible.

She wished she could freeze this moment in time, that she could stay right here in his arms. Only that notion was as foolish as falling in love with him was.

From their vantage point, she could see the rain in the distance, heading their way. Melancholy washed over her and she impatiently brushed it aside. Time enough for that later. For now, she intended to cherish every second.

"Ready?" Jake said. "We probably need to head out now if we're going to beat the rain."

"Sure. Thanks for bringing me here."

"It's one of my favorite places," he said. He leaped down from the boulder, landing on his feet. Goldie peered over the edge and her knees felt all wobbly. It seemed a whole lot farther looking down than it had going up.

"Jump and I'll catch you," he said. She hesitated. "I promise I won't let you fall."

She jumped and he caught her, laughing at her evident relief. "See, I told you I wouldn't let you fall."

Little did he know it was far too late for that. She'd fallen, all right. She'd fallen hard.

8

JAKE LAUGHED FROM sheer happiness as they reached the porch right ahead of the rain. "That was a close call."

Goldie rubbed her hands over her arms. "It's hard to believe May is this chilly. But then, I don't spend much time in the mountains, either."

"It's the mountains and the cold front bringing the rain." He opened the door for her. "Let's build another fire."

"Good idea."

Hmm. Another good idea would be lying in front of the fire with her naked. They went in and it was cozier inside than he could ever remember it being before—maybe it was the dampness outside, the sound of the rain on the roof, or having Goldie here with him. Thunder rumbled in the distance and she jumped slightly. He knew now how she felt about tornadoes. He couldn't control the weather, but he'd do damn near anything he could to keep her out of harm's way. "Are you okay?" he said, putting his arm around her.

She looked up at him and smiled. "It startled me but I'm fine. I feel safe with…well, here."

Jake had the impression that she'd almost said she felt safe with him. He pressed a kiss to her temple. "Let's get that fire started."

She eyed the dwindling supply of wood on the hearth. "Do you have more logs?"

"They're on the back porch—"

"I didn't even know there was a back porch."

"The door's sort of tucked into the back corner of the kitchen, past the table."

"If you want to bring in more logs, I'll lay the kindling."

They worked efficiently together. Jake hauled in varying sizes of firewood and Goldie had built an excellent fire. "Wow. I'm impressed."

"Girl scouts," she said with an easy smile.

"No kidding." He could see her in the uniform. Actually, he could see her in the uniform all grown up and it was hot. "I was a boy scout."

"Really? Did you do summer camps?"

They compared notes and realized that for three years they'd camped across the lake from one another for two weeks each June.

"Small world," Goldie said.

Jake struck a match to the kindling and it caught right away. "Nice fire, girl scout."

"Thanks." She stretched her hands out to capture the warmth and he wrapped his arms around her from behind.

"Still chilly?"

"I'll be warm in a minute."

"Hold that thought."

He sprinted down the hall, pulled a couple of blankets out of the closet, and returned to spread one on the floor in front of the fire. "Here you go. Have a seat." He sat and tugged her down to sit between his legs, wrapping the two of them in the other blanket. "Nothing like a little shared body heat to warm things up."

She leaned back into him, nestling her head between his shoulder and his jaw, her hair soft and fragrant against his skin. "Mmm. This is nice," she said.

From outside, thunder shook the cabin but Goldie didn't even flinch. Instead she brushed her thumb over the back of his wrist as if memorizing the feel of his skin against hers. "Jake…"

"Hmm?"

"When we were in bed last night…"

"Yeah?"

"You said you'd wanted to touch me like that from the first time you ever met me?"

Her unspoken question of *Why didn't you?* stretched between them.

"Baby, we both knew from the beginning we wanted different things from a relationship. I'll never, ever forget the way I felt the first time I saw you, when I walked up to Lauren's desk and there you were. I felt like the rug had been snatched out from under my feet. But it was clear what you were looking for, what I couldn't give you. I didn't think it was fair to either one of us."

"But this weekend has been—"

"Wonderful," he said, interrupting. "At least for me it has."

"That's exactly how I feel."

He smoothed his hand over the curve of her cheek, the line of her neck. "I never believed in love at first sight," he said, acknowledging to her at the same time what he was realizing himself. He loved her. "…before. That's why I worked so damn hard to stay away from you."

She turned to face him, kneeling in front of him, between his outstretched thighs, and linked her arms around his neck. "I looked at you and knew I'd never be the same again. So I went out of my way to avoid being around you."

Relief washed through him. She felt the same way. And she'd obviously decided her commitment requirement was over the top, otherwise she wouldn't sound so happy with the situation.

He cupped her buttocks in his hands, pulling her closer into his chest. She nuzzled at his neck and whispered, "I'm glad we couldn't avoid one another any longer."

"Not nearly as glad as I am," he said, working his hands up under the sweatshirt and T-shirt she wore to stroke the smooth lines of her back. "Are you warm yet? In my opinion you're wearing altogether too many clothes."

Smiling, she gripped the hems of both the T-shirt and the sweatshirt and pulled them over her head in one fell swoop. Her bare breasts were in tantalizing proximity of his mouth. "Better?"

"Much—" he lazily licked one nipple and it sprang to attention "—much—" he teased his tongue against the other tip and it tightened into a hard bud as well "—better."

"Take your shirt off," she ordered.

He complied, the cooler air settling against his skin.

She trailed her fingers through the hair on his chest. "I love your chest," she said as she fingered his nipples. He sucked in a harsh breath at the sensation that arrowed straight to his cock. Continuing her journey downward, she unerringly found his belt. "This is in the way. May I?"

"By all means."

Laughing softly under her breath, she undid his belt and then the button to his jeans. She pushed him lightly to his side and then his back. He stretched out and she worked his zipper down. He loved that she was as eager to get him out of his clothes as he was to have her naked. He lifted his hips and she tugged his jeans and underwear off together. "Now that's optimal," she said.

"Almost," he countered, tugging the drawstring on the

pajama pants she wore until they gave way. She wiggled out of them, leaving her gloriously nude.

He held out his hand. "Come here."

She came.

His last coherent thought as she straddled him was that he was the luckiest man alive.

GOLDIE STRETCHED LANGUIDLY, sated, her head pillowed on Jake's chest, his leg resting intimately between hers.

"Are you warm enough?" Jake said, stroking her back, pulling the blanket over the two of them.

"Mmm. I'm perfect." She'd never known such utter bliss. She snuggled closer to him. "That was perfect. It's amazing how different it was making love knowing you'd changed your mind, that we weren't on opposite sides of the fence any longer."

His hand stilled. Even though he didn't move, she could feel the shift in him, the tensing. An impending sense of doom descended on her. She raised onto one elbow and looked at him. She didn't want to see what she thought she was going to see.

"Jake?"

She felt him mentally withdrawing before he rolled to his side and scrubbed his hand through is hair. "Wait a second, honey. I haven't changed my stance. I thought you had. I never said I had."

"You thought I had? Never. I've never been less than crystal clear about how I felt on the subject."

"Me either," he said, his jaw taking on a stubborn set.

"But you knew how I felt, how important it is to me. So I thought you must have…" She trailed off, wrapping the blanket more firmly around her, a cold settling inside her that the fire couldn't possibly warm. She'd been naked numerous times with him but now she sat stripped emotionally, vulnerable. If he loved her, then he'd realize she needed to know he'd be there for her. The knowledge that he wouldn't even consider it cut her to shreds. She gathered her tattered emotions about her and strove for some measure of dignity. "I guess there's nothing left to say, is there?"

"What do you want? A proposal?"

It felt as if he'd backhanded her across the face. "Of course not. I just want the possibility of one. And with you, that's not even a remote chance." She hated herself, hated the neediness, but she couldn't seem to help tacking on what she shouldn't ask any more than she'd been able to not fall in love with him. "Is it?"

He pushed to his feet and stood naked before her. "I could lie to you. I could so easily say yes when I don't mean it, but there's no honor in that and it's not fair to either one of us. And I'd rather walk away from what we have right now than watch it slowly erode into what my parents have."

She wanted to tell him that it wouldn't. That she wouldn't let it. But she refused to beg him to love her. Because obviously he didn't. She'd been a fool to fall in love with him but she refused to compound her foolishness by selling herself and what was between them short. She shrugged, striving desperately not to show how her heart was breaking. "Then I guess we're back to square one."

He reached for her and she stepped back out of his range. "Don't. I think it's better if we just…don't." She drew a shaky breath. "We were both right. We knew this was impossible from the first time we met. I suggest we both forget this weekend ever happened, starting right now."

Sure, as if she could ever forget the taste of him in her mouth, the feel of him inside her.

"I agree."

"I have my paperwork in my satchel," she said, standing. With the blanket wrapped around her, she headed toward the hallway. "I'll just stay in Chad's room until the rain has stopped and you think the creek is passable."

"Fine."

The rain couldn't stop soon enough.

9

JAKE PACED THE FLOOR, silently cursing every decision he'd made in the last twenty-four hours, starting with the dumb-ass move of coming up here in the first place. If he hadn't come, then he wouldn't have found her in his bed. If he hadn't found her in his bed, he could've continued to avoid her. If he'd continued to avoid her, he wouldn't have made love to her and if he hadn't made love to her, he could've continued to pretend he hadn't fallen in love with her the first time he'd set eyes on her.

And now, dammit to hell, she was sequestered in Chad's room. The idea of her in any bedroom but his left him wanting to punch something, which was crazier than hell because he wasn't prone to either jealousy or violence.

He yanked on his jeans because he definitely looked crazier than hell pacing around the den naked as a jaybird. He resumed the therapeutic march from the fireplace to the recliners and back.

Why'd she have to be so damn stubborn? So unreasonable? Her way or the highway. He paused in his pacing… He was being equally unyielding, wasn't he? He started back—yeah, but his logic was, well, logical, reasonable. And it wasn't as if he hadn't met women before who weren't cool with his terms. The only problem was that he'd never been in love with any of them.

He heard the bedroom door open and Goldie appeared, heading toward the kitchen. Like a sucker punch to his gut, she was wearing one of Chad's button-downs, which fit her more like a dress than a shirt. "If you needed another T-shirt, you know where my closet is."

She shook her head without looking at him, "No. It's… I can't. It's just better this way." She pulled a bottled water out of the refrigerator. Without another word, she returned to the bedroom, closing the door firmly behind her. At least she didn't lock it. He supposed that was something.

He opened the front door and realized the rain had stopped. Thank God. The sooner it stopped, the sooner the creek would recede and the sooner they could get the hell out—

Not only had the rain stopped, but there was an eerie quiet to the moment. The only sound was the freight train…and there was no train line nearby. He spun, running hellbent for leather, yelling her name. "Goldie, get in the bathroom. Now. Tornado."

She stumbled out of the bedroom as he was about to fling the door open. He grabbed her, shoving her into the bathroom ahead of him. He lifted her into the tub, jumped in behind her and covered her body with his just as all the furies of hell descended on them in the form of a funnel cloud.

"It's over," Jake said, but she couldn't quite take it in. "Baby, quit shaking. It's over."

He moved from where he was crouching in the tub to sit on the edge, pulling her onto his lap. His hands shook as he stroked her head, her face, her back, her arms. "Are you okay? Are you hurt? Tell me you're okay. You've got to be okay. Nothing can happen to you."

She found her voice. "I'm fine. What about you?" Blood

dripped down into the tub. He was injured. "Oh, my God, you're bleeding. Where are you hurt?"

"I don't know. I don't care. Are you sure you're okay?"

The back of his right arm. His arm was bleeding. She looked around, for the first time seeing the rest of the room instead of just seeing Jake. The force of the wind had shattered the bathroom window. Obviously flying glass had caught the back of his arm. It could've been so much worse. She began to shake in earnest.

"What were you thinking throwing yourself on top of me like that? You could've been lower in the tub, more protected if you were beside me instead of on top of me." If a bigger piece of glass had caught him in the neck... Her voice escalated. "What were you thinking?" Then she was yelling because if she didn't yell, she thought she might cry. She could've lost him, forever. "What were you thinking?"

He yelled back, "That nothing could happen to you. You had to be safe."

There was a pause, and then they were desperately kissing one another. Jake scattered kisses over her face and she did the same, reassuring herself that he was whole and fine. He would've died for her. He would've died to keep her safe. How could anything ever prove how much he cared for her more than that?

"I love you," she said, gasping the words in between kisses.

"I couldn't stand it if I'd lost you. We'll get married tomorrow if you want to, but I never ever want to think of not having you with me again."

She needed him to know. "I don't need for you to marry me. I don't need that anymore."

"Oh, hell, no, you didn't just say that. You are the most ornery, contrary woman. Those were the first words I heard out of your mouth—that you wanted a husband. Then you were ready to dump me because I wouldn't talk long-term. And now, you're turning me down. I've got news for you, Goldilocks, I'll keep you here naked until you say yes."

"But I always thought my greatest fear was a tornado and I just realized it isn't. My biggest fear is losing you. I love you, regardless of the terms."

"Well, I've got news for you, Ms. Dawkins, the terms are we're getting hitched. Start thinking about a date."

"You're sure?"

"Never surer. There's something about thinking you might lose the woman you love in a natural disaster that puts things in perspective for a guy."

"Just think, if I hadn't shown up here and you hadn't found me in your bed, I might've never figured out that you were the guy who was just right for me."

AND AS THE REST OF this tale goes, Goldie and Jake went on to build their own little cabin in the woods, which became home to them and the baby they welcomed. Goldie, Jake and Baby became known as Papa Bear, Mama Bear and Baby Bear. And they all lived happily ever after....

* * * * *

Harlequin offers a romance for every mood!
See below for a sneak peek from our suspense romance line
Silhouette® Romantic Suspense.
Introducing HER HERO IN HIDING by
New York Times *bestselling author Rachel Lee.*

Kay Young returned to woozy consciousness to find that she was lying on a soft sofa beneath a heap of quilts near a cheerfully burning fire. When she tried to move, however, everything hurt, and she groaned.

At once she heard a sound, then a stranger with a hard, harsh face was squatting beside her. "Shh," he said softly. "You're safe here. I promise."

"I have to go," she said weakly, struggling against pain. "He'll find me. He can't find me."

"Easy, lady," he said quietly. "You're hurt. No one's going to find you here."

"He will," she said desperately, terror clutching at her insides. "He always finds me!"

"Easy," he said again. "There's a blizzard outside. No one's getting here tonight, not even the doctor. I know, because I tried."

"Doctor? I don't need a doctor! I've got to get away."

"There's nowhere to go tonight," he said levelly. "And if I thought you could stand, I'd take you to a window and show you."

But even as she tried once more to pull away the quilts, she remembered something else: this man had been gentle when he'd found her beside the road, even when she had kicked and clawed. He hadn't hurt her.

Terror receded just a bit. She looked at him and detected signs of true concern there.

The terror eased another notch and she let her head sag on the pillow. "He always finds me," she whispered.

"Not here. Not tonight. That much I can guarantee."

*Will Kay's mysterious rescuer protect her
from her worst fears?
Find out in HER HERO IN HIDING by* New York Times
*bestselling author Rachel Lee.
Available June 2010,
only from Silhouette® Romantic Suspense.*

HARLEQUIN® Romance®

Four friends, four dream weddings!

On a girly weekend in Las Vegas, best friends Alex, Molly, Serena and Jayne are supposed to just have fun and forget men, but they end up meeting their perfect matches! Will the love they find in Vegas stay in Vegas?

Find out in this sassy, fun and wildly romantic miniseries all about love and friendship!

Saving Cinderella! by MYRNA MACKENZIE
Available June

Vegas Pregnancy Surprise by SHIRLEY JUMP
Available July

Inconveniently Wed! by JACKIE BRAUN
Available August

Wedding Date with the Best Man
by MELISSA McCLONE
Available September

www.eHarlequin.com

HR17663

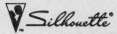

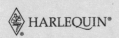

Showcase

On sale May 11, 2010

Reader favorites from the most talented voices in romance

Save $1.00 on the purchase of 1 or more Harlequin® Showcase books.

SAVE $1.00 on the purchase of 1 or more Harlequin® Showcase books.

Coupon expires Oct 31, 2010. Redeemable at participating retail outlets.
Limit one coupon per purchase. Valid in the U.S.A. and Canada only.

Canadian Retailers: Harlequin Enterprises Limited will pay the face value of this coupon plus 10.25¢ if submitted by customer for this product only. Any other use constitutes fraud. Coupon is nonassignable. Void if taxed, prohibited or restricted by law. Consumer must pay any government taxes. Void if copied. Nielsen Clearing House ("NCH") customers submit coupons and proof of sales to Harlequin Enterprises Limited, P.O. Box 3000, Saint John, NB E2L 4L3, Canada. Non-NCH retailer—for reimbursement submit coupons and proof of sales directly to Harlequin Enterprises Limited, Retail Marketing Department, 225 Duncan Mill Rd., Don Mills, ON M3B 3K9, Canada.

U.S. Retailers: Harlequin Enterprises Limited will pay the face value of this coupon plus 8¢ if submitted by customer for this product only. Any other use constitutes fraud. Coupon is nonassignable. Void if taxed, prohibited or restricted by law. Consumer must pay any government taxes. Void if copied. For reimbursement submit coupons and proof of sales directly to Harlequin Enterprises Limited, P.O. Box 880478, El Paso, TX 88588-0478, U.S.A. Cash value 1/100 cents.

52609015

5 65373 00076 2   (8100)0 11651

® and TM are trademarks owned and used by the trademark owner and/or its licensee.
© 2009 Harlequin Enterprises Limited

HSCCOUP0410

Love Inspired®

Bestselling author

JILLIAN HART

brings you another heartwarming story
from

the
GRANGER
FAMILY
RANCH

Rancher Justin Granger hasn't seen his high school sweetheart
since she rode out of town with his heart. Now she's back, with
sadness in her eyes, seeking a job as his cook and housekeeper.
He agrees but is determined to avoid her...until he discovers
that her big dream has always been him!

The Rancher's Promise

*Available June
wherever books are sold.*

REQUEST YOUR FREE BOOKS!

2 FREE NOVELS
PLUS 2
FREE GIFTS!

HARLEQUIN®

Blaze

Red-hot reads!

YES! Please send me 2 FREE Harlequin® Blaze™ novels and my 2 FREE gifts (gifts are worth about $10). After receiving them, if I don't wish to receive any more books, I can return the shipping statement marked "cancel." If I don't cancel, I will receive 6 brand-new novels every month and be billed just $4.24 per book in the U.S. or $4.71 per book in Canada. That's a saving of at least 15% off the cover price. It's quite a bargain. Shipping and handling is just 50¢ per book.* I understand that accepting the 2 free books and gifts places me under no obligation to buy anything. I can always return a shipment and cancel at any time. Even if I never buy another book, the two free books and gifts are mine to keep forever.

151/351 HDN E5LS

Name	(PLEASE PRINT)	
Address		Apt. #
City	State/Prov.	Zip/Postal Code

Signature (if under 18, a parent or guardian must sign)

Mail to the **Harlequin Reader Service**:
IN U.S.A.: P.O. Box 1867, Buffalo, NY 14240-1867
IN CANADA: P.O. Box 609, Fort Erie, Ontario L2A 5X3

Not valid for current subscribers to Harlequin Blaze books.

Want to try two free books from another line?
Call 1-800-873-8635 or visit www.morefreebooks.com.

* Terms and prices subject to change without notice. Prices do not include applicable taxes. N.Y. residents add applicable sales tax. Canadian residents will be charged applicable provincial taxes and GST. Offer not valid in Quebec. This offer is limited to one order per household. All orders subject to approval. Credit or debit balances in a customer's account(s) may be offset by any other outstanding balance owed by or to the customer. Please allow 4 to 6 weeks for delivery. Offer available while quantities last.

Your Privacy: Harlequin Books is committed to protecting your privacy. Our Privacy Policy is available online at www.eHarlequin.com or upon request from the Reader Service. From time to time we make our lists of customers available to reputable third parties who may have a product or service of interest to you. If you would prefer we not share your name and address, please check here. ☐

Help us get it right—We strive for accurate, respectful and relevant communications. To clarify or modify your communication preferences, visit us at www.ReaderService.com/consumerchoice.

HB10R

HARLEQUIN® *Blaze*™

is proud to present

New York Times bestselling author

Vicki Lewis Thompson

with a brand-new trilogy,
SONS OF CHANCE
**where three sexy brothers
meet three irresistible women.**

Look for the first book
WANTED!

*Available beginning in June 2010
wherever books are sold.*

red-hot reads

www.eHarlequin.com

HB79548